THE BLACKMAILER'S BARGAIN

ARABELLA LARKSPUR

CHAPTER 1

The letter arrived on a Tuesday morning, just as the autumn rain began to tap against the drawing room windows of Belmont House. Poppy Hartwell looked up from her needlework as Jenkins, their elderly butler, approached with the morning post arranged on a silver tray.

"The post, Miss Hartwell," he said, his voice carrying the same measured tone it had possessed for the past twenty years.

Poppy set aside her embroidery and reached for the small stack of correspondence. Most of it would be the usual collection of invitations and calling cards—the tedious social obligations that filled the days of a lady of her standing. But as her fingers sorted through the envelopes, one caught her attention immediately.

It bore no sender's name, no return address. The paper was of good quality, but the handwriting was unfamiliar—a careful, deliberate script that seemed to avoid any identifying flourishes. Her name was written in black ink across the cream-coloured envelope: *Miss P. Hartwell.*

Something about it made her pause. She glanced around the drawing room, taking in the familiar comfort of her surroundings. The portraits of long-dead Hartwells gazed down from the walls, their stern faces offering no counsel. Her mother's delicate china figurines caught the grey light from the windows, casting small shadows across the mahogany side table.

Poppy broke the wax seal and unfolded the single sheet of paper within.

Miss Hartwell,

I write to inform you that certain documents have come into my possession—documents which I believe you would prefer remained private. Some personal papers of your father's, in particular, contain passages which would prove most illuminating to society, should they become public knowledge.

I am not an unreasonable person. A modest sum

would ensure these materials remain safely in my keeping, away from prying eyes and wagging tongues. I shall contact you again soon with specific arrangements.

I trust you understand the delicate nature of this matter and will give it your urgent consideration.

A Concerned Party

The letter fluttered in Poppy's suddenly trembling hands. She read it again, each word striking her like a physical blow. Her father's personal papers. She had thought them safely locked away, buried with the man himself these past three years.

The drawing room door opened, and her younger sister Rose swept in, her face bright with excitement.

"Poppy, you'll never guess—" Rose stopped mid-sentence, her smile fading as she took in her sister's pale complexion. "Whatever is the matter? You look as though you've seen a ghost."

Poppy quickly folded the letter, her mind racing. Rose was twenty-two, beautiful, and utterly untouched by the shadows that had fallen across the Hartwell name. In just three weeks, she was to be married to the Honourable James Whitmore, a match that would restore some measure of respectability to their family. A marriage that could be destroyed in an instant if the wrong secrets came to light.

"Nothing at all," Poppy managed, forcing a smile. "Just some correspondence that requires attention. You were saying?"

Rose's expression remained concerned, but she allowed herself to be diverted. "The final fitting for my wedding dress has been moved to Friday. Mrs Pemberton thinks the sleeves need adjusting." She moved closer, studying Poppy's face. "Are you quite certain you're well? You've gone terribly pale."

"I'm perfectly fine." Poppy rose from her chair, the letter clutched tightly in her hand. "I think I'll just step out for some air. The rain seems to be letting up."

But as Rose chattered on about dress fittings and flower arrangements, Poppy's thoughts were consumed by a single, terrifying question: what exactly was in those papers of her father's?

She excused herself and retreated to her private sitting room, a small chamber on the second floor that had been her sanctuary since childhood. Here, surrounded by her books and personal mementoes, she tried to think clearly about what the letter might mean.

Her father, Sir Charles Hartwell, had been a

respected member of Parliament until his sudden death three years ago. But his final years had been marked by whispers and speculation—rumours of financial irregularities, questions about his business dealings, suggestions that all was not as it seemed with the Hartwell fortune. Nothing had ever been proven, and his death had brought a merciful end to the gossip. But if there were papers, if he had written down things that should have remained secret...

The sound of footsteps in the corridor made her hastily tuck the letter into her desk drawer. Her mother appeared in the doorway, leaning heavily on her walking stick. Lady Catherine Hartwell had aged considerably since her husband's death, her once-vibrant spirit dimmed by grief and ill health.

"Poppy, dear, I was wondering if you might join me for luncheon. Rose has gone to see her dress-maker, and I find myself rather lonely."

"Of course, Mama." Poppy rose quickly, her heart clenching at the fragility in her mother's voice. Lady Catherine's health had never fully recovered from the strain of her husband's final months. The scandal of those days—the whispered accusations, the cold shoulders from former friends—had taken a terrible toll. Another shock, another disgrace, might well prove more than she could bear.

As they made their way downstairs together, Poppy's mind churned with possibilities. She could ignore the letter, of course, pretend it had never arrived. But blackmailers were rarely deterred by silence. They were like vultures, circling their prey with infinite patience.

She could pay whatever sum was demanded. But that path led only to endless demands, an ever-deepening spiral of payments that would eventually drain what remained of the family's resources.

Or she could fight back. But how did one fight an enemy who remained hidden in the shadows?

Over a quiet luncheon of soup and cold meats, Poppy watched her mother carefully. Lady Catherine spoke of small domestic matters—the gardener's concerns about the rose bushes, a letter from her sister in Bath—but Poppy could see the effort it cost her. Dark circles shadowed her eyes, and her hands trembled slightly as she lifted her teacup.

"Mama," Poppy said gently, "Dr Morrison said you should be getting more rest."

"Oh, doctors," Lady Catherine waved a dismissive hand. "They're always prescribing rest. As if rest could cure every ailment." But her smile was wan, and she set down her cup with obvious fatigue.

After luncheon, Poppy helped her mother to her bedroom for an afternoon nap. As she tucked the quilts around the older woman's frail form, Lady Catherine caught her hand.

"You're a good daughter, Poppy. I don't know what Rose and I would do without you."

The words were like a knife in Poppy's heart. How could she explain that her very presence might be what brought disaster upon them all?

Once her mother was settled, Poppy returned to her sitting room and retrieved the letter from her desk drawer. She read it again, searching for any clue about the identity of her blackmailer. But the writing revealed nothing, and the paper bore no watermark or other distinguishing features.

She moved to the window and stared out at the garden, where the last of the summer flowers were surrendering to autumn's chill. Somewhere out there, someone knew her father's secrets. Someone who believed those secrets were worth exploiting.

Her father's study had been locked since his death, the key kept safe in her possession. She had been through his desk when settling the estate, and while she had found a journal, there had been nothing else that had drawn her attention. If there been something else, some other papers, she hadn't seen them, so where were they now? And more importantly, what did they contain?

A soft knock at the door interrupted her brooding. "Come in," she called.

Jenkins appeared, carrying a tea tray. "I thought you might care for some refreshment, Miss."

"Thank you, Jenkins." She accepted the tea gratefully, noting the butler's kind but observant gaze. Jenkins had served the family faithfully through all their trials. If anyone understood the weight of keeping secrets, it was he.

"Jenkins," she said carefully, "do you recall my father having any kind of collection of personal papers or documents? Anything other than his journal?"

The elderly man considered the question thoughtfully. "I believe Sir Charles did keep records of some sort, Miss. He was often writing in the evenings, in his study. But I couldn't say what became of such papers after..." He paused delicately.

"After he died," Poppy finished. "No, of course not. Thank you, Jenkins."

When the butler had gone, Poppy found herself facing a stark choice. She could continue to wait and worry, allowing the blackmailer to dictate the terms of this deadly game. Or she could take action.

But what sort of action? She was a spinster of twenty-eight, with no husband to protect her and no male relatives to advise her. Rose was too young and innocent to burden with such knowledge, and their mother too fragile to withstand another scandal.

She thought of their social circle—the ladies who had once called regularly, the gentlemen who had once sought her father's counsel. How many would stand by them if the worst came to light? How many would simply turn away, as so many had done during those final, difficult months before her father's death?

The afternoon light was fading when Poppy finally made her decision. She could not face this alone. She needed help—professional help from someone who understood the law and the ways of men who traded in secrets and threats.

But who could she trust with such a delicate matter? The family solicitor, Mr Pemberton, was elderly and conservative, likely to advise patience and payment rather than confrontation, but still he was the only one she knew that she could turn to who might possibly help. She needed someone with experience in fighting such battles, someone who would not be shocked by whatever secrets her father might have committed to paper and maybe Mr Pemberton would know someone.

As the first stars appeared in the darkening sky, Poppy sat down at her writing desk and took up her pen. Somewhere in London, there had to be someone who could help her. Someone with the knowledge and courage to stand against the forces that threatened her family.

She would not surrender without a fight. Whatever her father had done, whatever secrets lay buried in those missing journals, she would find a way to protect the people she loved.

The letter had been only the beginning. But it would not be the end.

As she began to write, Poppy felt a strange mixture of fear and determination settle over her. The game had begun, and she would play it to win—no matter what the cost might be.

CHAPTER 2

The offices of Pemberton, Wickham & Associates occupied a narrow Georgian building on Lincoln's Inn Fields, its soot-darkened facade bearing the weight of decades of legal deliberations. Poppy stood before the familiar brass nameplate, gathering her courage before ascending the worn stone steps.

She had visited Mr Pemberton many times over the years—first as a child accompanying her father, then later to settle the estate after Sir Charles's death. The elderly solicitor had always been kindness itself, treating her with the sort of paternal concern that had made her feel safe in an uncertain world. But today's visit would test the bounds of that protective relationship.

The clerk showed her into Mr Pemberton's office, where the old gentleman rose from behind his mahogany desk with obvious pleasure.

"My dear Miss Hartwell, what a delightful surprise. Please, do sit down. Shall I ring for tea?"

"Thank you, Mr Pemberton. That would be most welcome."

As the solicitor bustled about arranging refreshments, Poppy took in the familiar surroundings. The office had not changed in twenty years—the same leather-bound volumes lined the walls, the same faded Persian carpet covered the floor, the same portrait of some long-dead legal luminary gazed down from above the fireplace. There was something deeply reassuring about this continuity, this sense that some things, at least, remained constant in a shifting world.

"Now then," Mr Pemberton said, settling himself behind his desk once more, "what brings you to see me? I do hope there are no difficulties with the estate settlement?"

Poppy accepted her teacup with hands that trembled only slightly. "Not exactly, Mr Pemberton. Though the matter I wish to discuss does concern my father's affairs."

The solicitor's expression grew more attentive. "Indeed? How may I be of assistance?"

For a moment, Poppy hesitated. Once she spoke the words aloud, there would be no taking them back. But the memory of her mother's fragile health and Rose's radiant happiness as she planned her wedding strengthened her resolve.

"I have received a letter," she began carefully, "from someone claiming to possess certain documents belonging to my late father. Documents which, this person suggests, might prove embarrassing if made public."

Mr Pemberton's teacup rattled against its saucer as he set it down rather abruptly. "My dear Miss Hartwell, are you saying you are being blackmailed?"

"I believe that is the correct term, yes."

The elderly solicitor leaned back in his chair, his face grave. "This is a most serious matter indeed. May I ask what sort of documents this person claims to possess?"

"Some kind of personal papers, apparently. My father's personal papers."

"I see." Mr Pemberton steepled his fingers beneath his chin, a gesture Poppy remembered from her childhood. "And what demands have been made?"

"None yet, specifically. The letter merely suggested that a 'modest sum' would ensure the documents remained private. I was told to expect further communication."

"Most concerning." The solicitor rose and began to pace slowly about the room. "Miss Hartwell, I must ask—are you aware of any... irregularities in your father's affairs that might provide ammunition for such a scheme?"

Poppy felt heat rise in her cheeks. "You were his solicitor, Mr Pemberton. Surely you would know better than I."

"Quite so, quite so." He paused in his pacing. "Your father was always most proper in his business dealings, at least in those matters which came before me. But there were areas of his life—his political activities, certain financial ventures—where he sought counsel elsewhere."

"What would you advise?" Poppy asked. "Should I simply pay whatever sum is demanded?"

Poppy watched as Mr Pemberton's expression grew troubled and then drew a sharp breath in surprise at his next words.

"My dear child, that would be most inadvisable. Blackmailers are rarely satisfied with a single payment. They are more like... well, like leeches.

Once they attach themselves, they continue to drain their victim until nothing remains."

"Then what alternative do I have?"

The solicitor resumed his seat, his fingers drumming nervously on the desk. "There are legal remedies, of course. Blackmail is a serious crime. But pursuing such a course would require making the matter public, which rather defeats the purpose of preventing scandal."

Poppy's heart sank. "So you're saying there's nothing to be done?"

"Not nothing, precisely. But the options are... limited." He paused, seeming to wrestle with some internal debate. "Miss Hartwell, I wonder if I might mention a name to you. A gentleman who might be better equipped to handle such a delicate situation."

"A gentleman?"

"A barrister, actually. Or rather, a former barrister. Mr Edward Taverner." Mr Pemberton's voice carried a note of hesitation. "He was once considered one of the finest legal minds of his generation. Brilliant, absolutely brilliant. But..."

"But?"

"Well, his career came to rather an abrupt end some years ago. A matter of professional disgrace,

I'm afraid. There were allegations of impropriety, though nothing was ever proven conclusively."

Poppy leaned forward in her chair. "What sort of impropriety?"

"It's rather difficult to explain without going into tedious legal details. Suffice it to say that Mr Taverner was involved in a case that went very badly indeed. There were suggestions that he had... well, that he had not been entirely honest with the court. His reputation was destroyed overnight."

"And you think this disgraced barrister would be willing to help me?"

Mr Pemberton shifted uncomfortably. "The thing is, Miss Hartwell, Mr Taverner's own fall from grace involved matters not entirely dissimilar to your current predicament. He was fighting powerful men who preferred their secrets to remain buried. In the end, those men won, and Mr Taverner paid the price."

"Where is he now?"

"He retired to his family estate in Norfolk. Taverner Hall, I believe it's called. A rather remote place, by all accounts. He lives there with his sister-in-law, Lady Agnes Taverner. They keep very much to themselves."

Poppy considered this information carefully. A

disgraced barrister living in seclusion hardly sounded like the sort of ally she needed. And yet...

"You believe he might understand my situation?"

"I believe," Mr Pemberton said slowly, "that Mr Taverner has experience with the sort of enemies you may be facing. And I believe he has reasons of his own to despise those who traffic in secrets and lies."

"Would he see me, do you think?"

"That I cannot say. He has refused all visitors for several years now. But..." The solicitor opened a drawer and withdrew a sheet of paper. "I could provide you with his direction, should you wish to write to him."

Poppy watched as he carefully wrote out an address in his precise hand. "Mr Pemberton, may I ask why you're suggesting this course of action? Surely there must be other barristers in London who could advise me?"

The old gentleman's expression grew sad. "My dear child, the sort of men who engage in blackmail are rarely ordinary criminals. They are often connected to powerful interests, protected by wealth and influence. Most respectable barristers would be reluctant to challenge such forces, particularly in a case involving... well, involving a lady's reputation."

"But Mr Taverner would be different?"

"Mr Taverner has nothing left to lose. And in my experience, Miss Hartwell, that can make a man either very dangerous or very useful. In this case, I suspect it might be both."

Poppy took the paper from his hand, noting the address: Taverner Hall, near Wymondham, Norfolk. It seemed impossibly remote, a world away from the drawing rooms of London society.

"There is one other thing," Mr Pemberton said quietly. "If you do decide to contact Mr Taverner, you should be prepared for the possibility that he may refuse to help. His experiences have left him... well, somewhat bitter toward the world. And he has particular reason to distrust anyone connected to the sort of society circles your family moves in."

"What do you mean?"

"The case that destroyed his career involved certain members of Parliament. Men of influence and power who did not appreciate his efforts to expose their misconduct. Your father, being an MP himself..." He spread his hands helplessly.

Poppy felt a chill run down her spine. "Are you suggesting my father was involved in Mr Taverner's disgrace?"

"Not directly, no. But the political world is a

small one, Miss Hartwell. Mr Taverner might well view any member of that world—or their families—with suspicion."

They sat in silence for a moment, the weight of this revelation settling between them. Finally, Poppy folded the paper carefully and placed it in her reticule.

"Thank you for your counsel, Mr Pemberton. I shall consider what you've told me very carefully."

"I hope I have not overstepped in suggesting such a course. It's simply that ordinary legal channels seem inadequate for your particular difficulty."

As Poppy prepared to leave, the solicitor caught her hand gently.

"Miss Hartwell, I feel I must warn you once more. The path you are contemplating is not without its own dangers. Mr Taverner is not... well, he is not the sort of gentleman you are accustomed to dealing with. And if you do succeed in engaging his help, you may find yourself drawn into battles you never intended to fight."

"Thank you for the warning," Poppy replied. "But I'm afraid the battle has already begun, whether I intended it or not."

The journey back to Belmont House passed in a blur of crowded omnibuses and jostling pedestrians.

Poppy's mind was consumed with what she had learned. A disgraced barrister living in exile, a man with his own reasons to hate the powerful forces that might be behind her blackmailer's threats. It seemed like the stuff of sensation novels rather than real life.

But as she climbed the front steps of her family home, she was reminded of what was at stake. Through the drawing room window, she could see Rose and her mother taking tea together, their faces bright with animated conversation about wedding preparations. They looked so happy, so untouched by the shadows that were gathering around them.

That evening, after Rose had retired to bed and her mother had been settled for the night, Poppy sat at her writing desk in the privacy of her sitting room. The address Mr Pemberton had given her lay before her, along with a sheet of her finest writing paper.

How did one approach a man who had been destroyed by scandal? How did one ask for help from someone who had every reason to despise her family's social position?

She dipped her pen in ink and began to write, choosing each word with careful deliberation:

Mr Taverner,

I write to you on the recommendation of Mr Pemberton of Lincoln's Inn, who suggested you might be able to offer counsel in a matter of some delicacy. I find myself in circumstances which require the advice of someone with experience in... unconventional legal difficulties.

I would be most grateful for the opportunity to consult with you, should you be willing to receive a visitor. I understand that your time is valuable and your privacy important, but I assure you that my need is genuine and urgent.

I remain, sir, your most obedient servant,

Miss P. Hartwell

She read the letter over several times, weighing each phrase. It was formal enough to be respectful, yet vague enough to avoid revealing too much in case it fell into the wrong hands. Most importantly, it contained nothing that might immediately prejudice him against her cause.

With a hand that trembled only slightly, she folded the letter, sealed it with wax, and addressed it to Edward Taverner, Esquire, Taverner Hall, Norfolk.

Tomorrow, she would post it and begin the anxious wait for a reply. Tonight, she could only hope that somewhere in the remote Norfolk countryside, there lived a man willing to help a stranger fight the demons of her father's past.

The die was cast. Whatever came next, she would face it with courage, for the sake of those she loved most in the world.

CHAPTER 3

The reply came three days later, delivered by the afternoon post in an envelope bearing the Taverner family crest. Poppy's hands trembled as she broke the seal, half-expecting a curt refusal. Instead, she found a single sheet of paper containing just a few lines written in a bold, angular hand:

Miss Hartwell,

You may call upon me at Taverner Hall on Thursday next at three o'clock. Come prepared to speak plainly. I have little patience for social niceties or feminine vapours.

E. Taverner

Post Scriptum: The journey from London requires an overnight stay. Mrs Pembroke at the village inn can provide suitable accommodation.

Poppy read the letter twice, uncertain whether to be relieved or alarmed by its brusque tone. There was no warmth in the words, no courtesy beyond the bare minimum required by civilized correspondence. Yet he had agreed to see her, which was more than she had dared hope.

Rose looked up from her embroidery as Poppy entered the morning room. "You've been receiving rather a lot of correspondence lately. Nothing troubling, I hope?"

"Nothing at all," Poppy replied, folding the letter carefully. "Simply some business matters that require attention."

"How dreadfully dull for you." Rose resumed her stitching with the easy dismissal of someone who had never needed to concern herself with anything more taxing than choosing ribbons for her bonnet. "James says that once we're married, I shall never need to trouble myself with such tedious affairs. He'll manage everything."

Poppy felt a pang of something that might have been envy. How simple life must seem when one could rely entirely upon a husband's protection. But even as the thought crossed her mind, she dismissed it. She had seen too much of marriage among their acquaintances to believe it offered any true security. Men could die, leaving their widows helpless. They could prove foolish with money, or cruel in private, or simply absent when most needed.

"That will be very comfortable for you," she said aloud, settling into the chair opposite her sister.

"Speaking of which," Rose continued, "James has suggested we take our wedding trip to the Lake District. He says the scenery is quite sublime in autumn. Of course, we shall have to return before Christmas, as his mother is most particular about family gatherings."

As Rose chattered on about wedding plans and honeymoon arrangements, Poppy's mind wandered to the journey she herself would soon undertake. Norfolk was a considerable distance from London, requiring an early morning departure by railway and then a lengthy carriage ride across unfamiliar countryside. The prospect filled her with both apprehension and a strange sort of excitement.

She had lived her entire life within the safe boundaries of London society, venturing no farther than Bath or Brighton for the occasional holiday. The idea of travelling alone to meet a complete stranger—a disgraced stranger, at that—would have horrified her mother and scandalized their neighbours. But circumstances had moved far beyond the realm of conventional propriety.

Thursday morning dawned grey and misty, with the promise of rain hanging heavy in the air. Poppy had told her mother she was visiting an old school friend in the country—a lie that sat uncomfortably on her conscience but seemed preferable to the complex explanations the truth would require.

Rose had offered to accompany her, but Poppy had demurred, claiming her friend was still in mourning and preferred to receive only one visitor at a time. The deception came so easily that it frightened her a little. When had she become so adept at concealing her true activities?

The railway carriage was crowded with commercial travellers and country folk, none of whom paid any attention to the quietly dressed young woman in the corner seat. Poppy watched the London suburbs give way to open countryside, feeling as though she were leaving behind not just her home but her entire identity. The woman who boarded this train was no longer simply Miss Hartwell of Belmont House, beloved daughter and devoted sister. She was someone else entirely—someone capable of secrets and subterfuge, someone willing to venture into unknown territory in pursuit of dangerous knowledge.

The journey to Wymondham took the better part of the day, with changes at Cambridge and Norwich that left Poppy feeling travel-worn and slightly over-whelmed. By the time she reached the village inn where Mr Taverner had suggested she lodge, the autumn evening was drawing in, and she was grateful for the warm glow spilling from the inn's windows.

Mrs Pembroke proved to be a motherly woman with kind eyes and flour-dusted hands, who fussed over Poppy's arrival and insisted on providing a substantial supper despite her guest's protests that she was too nervous to eat.

"Nonsense, dear," the innkeeper's wife declared, setting down a plate of roasted beef and vegetables. "A young lady travelling alone needs her strength. Are you quite certain your family knows where you are? It's most unusual for a lady of your quality to be wandering about Norfolk unaccompanied."

"I'm visiting... a family friend," Poppy managed, the lie becoming more uncomfortable with each repetition.

"Ah, well, I suppose that's different then. Though I can't think of many gentry families hereabouts who might be entertaining visitors from London. Most of the great houses have been empty for years, what with the agricultural difficulties and all."

After supper, Poppy retired to her small but comfortable chamber, where she lay awake for hours listening to the unfamiliar sounds of the country-side. Somewhere in the distance, an owl called repeatedly, its haunting cry seeming to echo her own sense of uncertainty about what the morrow might bring.

When morning finally came, she dressed with particular care, choosing her most respectable trav-elling dress and arranging her hair in a severe style that she hoped would lend her an air of serious purpose. Whatever Mr Taverner's opinion of her sex might be, she was determined to prove herself worthy of his time and attention.

The hired carriage that would take her to Taverner Hall arrived punctually at half past two, driven by a taciturn man who seemed disinclined to conversation. As they rolled through the Norfolk countryside, Poppy found herself increasingly impressed by the wild beauty of the landscape. Here were no carefully tended gardens or manicured parks, but rather an untamed realm of ancient trees and rolling hills that spoke of centuries of uninterrupted solitude.

"That be Taverner Hall ahead, miss," the driver announced as they crested a small rise.

Poppy leaned forward eagerly, then fell back in her seat with a sharp intake of breath. The building that sprawled before them could indeed be called a hall, but it bore little resemblance to the grand country houses she had visited in her youth. Taverner Hall was a Gothic monstrosity of grey stone and black timber, its towers and battlements creating a jagged silhouette against the leaden sky.

More shocking still was its obvious state of decay. Ivy had claimed large portions of the facade, windows gaped dark and broken in several places, and what had once been formal gardens now ran wild with weeds and brambles. It was like something from one of the sensation novels Rose favoured—the sort of place where mysterious disappearances occurred and family curses came to pass.

"Are you quite certain this is the correct address?" Poppy asked faintly.

"Aye, this be Taverner Hall right enough," the driver replied with what might have been satisfaction. "Though it ain't what it once was, I'll grant you that."

As they approached the main entrance, Poppy could see that someone had made token efforts to maintain the immediate surroundings. The drive, while pitted with holes, had been recently cleared of fallen branches, and the massive oak door that fronted the building appeared to be in good repair. But these small concessions to civilization only served to emphasize the overall atmosphere of abandonment and decay.

The carriage drew to a halt, and Poppy found herself staring up at the imposing entrance with considerable trepidation. Gargoyles leered down from the stone archway above the door, their expressions seeming to mirror her own sense of unease. What sort of man chose to live in such a place?

Before she could lose her nerve entirely, the great door swung open to reveal a tall figure silhouetted against the dim interior. Even at a distance, she could see that this must be Edward Taverner himself —the breadth of his shoulders and the confident way he held himself spoke of someone accustomed to command, despite his current reduced circumstances.

"Miss Hartwell, I presume," he called out, his voice carrying clearly across the forecourt. "You're punctual. I appreciate that in any person, but particularly in a woman."

There was something in his tone that suggested this was not necessarily a compliment. Poppy gathered her skirts and descended from the carriage, acutely conscious of being observed and measured. As she drew nearer, she could make out more details of her host's appearance.

Edward Taverner was a man of perhaps forty years, with dark hair that showed threads of premature silver and eyes of such a pale blue they seemed almost colourless. His features were aristocratic but harsh, as though life had carved them from unyielding stone. He was dressed simply in country clothes that had seen better days, but he wore them with an air of casual authority that spoke of good breeding despite his current circumstances.

"Mr Taverner," she replied, offering a slight curtsey. "Thank you for agreeing to see me."

He studied her for a moment with those unsettling pale eyes, his expression giving away nothing of his thoughts. "We shall see whether you have reason to thank me when our business is concluded. Come inside—the afternoon grows chill, and I have no intention of conducting this interview on my doorstep."

The interior of Taverner Hall proved to be every bit as unsettling as its exterior suggested. The entrance hall soared to a vaulted ceiling lost in shadows, its walls lined with portraits of long-dead Taverners who gazed down with expressions of stern disapproval. Dust motes danced in the weak light that filtered through tall, narrow windows, and the air carried the musty scent of a house that had seen better days.

"I hope the journey was not too taxing," Taverner said as he led her across the stone floor, their footsteps echoing in the vast space. "Country travel can be trying for those accustomed to London's conveniences."

"Not at all," Poppy replied, though in truth she was beginning to feel rather overwhelmed by her surroundings. "The countryside is quite... dramatic."

"That's one word for it." There was a note of dry amusement in his voice. "My late brother used to say that Norfolk was God's way of reminding Englishmen that beauty and comfort need not go hand in hand."

They passed through a series of increasingly dilapidated rooms, each more depressing than the last. Furniture stood shrouded in dust sheets like so many ghosts, and more than one window showed evidence of recent repairs with wooden boards rather than glass. It was clear that while Mr Taverner might maintain some pretence of genteel living, his resources were severely limited.

At last, they arrived at what appeared to be a library, though many of the shelves stood empty and those books that remained seemed to be in poor condition. A fire burned in the massive stone fire-place, providing the first real warmth Poppy had felt since entering the house.

"Pray be seated," Taverner said, indicating a chair that had been placed near the fire. "And tell me, Miss Hartwell, what desperate circumstances have driven you to seek assistance from a man of my diminished reputation?"

The question was delivered with such blunt directness that Poppy found herself momentarily speechless. She had expected some preliminary courtesies, some gentle inquiry into her background and family connections. Instead, she was confronted with a demand for immediate honesty that left her feeling exposed and uncertain.

"I... that is..." she began, then stopped herself and took a steadying breath. If he wanted plain speaking, then plain speaking he should have. "I am being blackmailed, Mr Taverner. Someone claims to possess my late father's private journals and threatens to make them public unless I pay for their silence."

For the first time since her arrival, Edward Taverner's expression showed genuine interest rather than mere polite attention.

"Indeed? And what precisely do these journals contain that makes them worth concealing?"

"I don't know," Poppy admitted. "That's rather the problem."

Before Taverner could respond, the library door opened to admit a woman Poppy had not heard approaching. She was perhaps fifty years of age, dressed entirely in black, with silver hair pulled back in a severe style that emphasized the sharp angles of her face. There was something about her bearing that suggested nobility, though like everything else in this house, it seemed touched by decline and sorrow.

"Agnes," Taverner said without turning around, "allow me to present Miss Hartwell. Miss Hartwell, my aunt, Lady Agnes Taverner."

The woman's dark eyes fixed on Poppy with an intensity that was almost physical. "So," she said in a voice like silk over steel, "you are the young woman who has brought my nephew out of his hermitage. How... interesting."

There was something in Lady Agnes's tone that made Poppy profoundly uncomfortable, though she could not quite identify what it was. The woman continued to study her with those penetrating dark eyes, as though seeking to peer into her very soul.

"Agnes is the mistress of Taverner Hall," Edward explained, seemingly oblivious to the undercurrents swirling around them. "She manages our domestic arrangements with admirable efficiency."

"Such as they are," Lady Agnes murmured, moving to stand beside the fireplace. "We do not often entertain visitors, Miss Hartwell. Indeed, you are the first guest we have received in... how long, Edward? Two years? Three?"

"I'm honoured by your hospitality," Poppy managed, though she was beginning to wonder if accepting Taverner's invitation had been a mistake.

"Honour," Lady Agnes repeated softly. "Yes, I suppose that is one way to look at it."

As the three of them stood there in the firelight, surrounded by the shadows and dust of the decaying hall, Poppy felt a chill that had nothing to do with the autumn air seeping through the ancient walls.

She had come here seeking help in solving her family's crisis, but she was beginning to suspect that Taverner Hall harboured secrets of its own—secrets that might prove far more dangerous than anything contained in her father's missing papers.

CHAPTER 4

The evening air in the library grew thick with unspoken tensions as Lady Agnes glided from the room as silently as she had entered, leaving Poppy alone with Edward Taverner. The fire crackled in the grate, casting dancing shadows across his angular features as he settled into the chair opposite hers.

"Now then," he said, his pale eyes fixed intently upon her face, "let us dispense with pleasantries and speak of practical matters. You say you are being blackmailed over some papers of your fathers, but you claim ignorance of their contents. That strikes me as remarkably naive, Miss Hartwell."

Poppy bristled at his tone. "I assure you, Mr Taverner, I am not in the habit of prying into private correspondence, even that of deceased family members."

"How admirably proper of you." His voice carried a note of dry sarcasm that made her cheeks burn. "And yet here you sit in the parlour of a disgraced barrister, having travelled halfway across England to seek assistance from a man whose very name is synonymous with professional ruin. One might question whether propriety is truly your primary concern."

The observation stung because it contained more than a grain of truth. A proper young lady would have accepted Mr Pemberton's advice to pay the blackmailer and hope for the best. She would not have embarked upon this wild venture into the Norfolk countryside to consult with a man of questionable reputation.

"My family's welfare is my primary concern," she replied with as much dignity as she could muster. "If that requires me to set aside certain... conventions, then so be it."

"Ah." Edward leaned back in his chair, a ghost of a smile playing about his lips. "There's the steel beneath the silk. I wondered if it existed."

Before Poppy could formulate a response to this

cryptic comment, he continued speaking, his tone becoming more businesslike.

"The difficulty with your situation, Miss Hartwell, is that any investigation into these missing papers will necessarily draw attention to their contents. If we are to discover who possesses them and what leverage they hope to gain, we must be prepared to move freely within society circles—to ask questions, cultivate sources, and generally conduct ourselves as people with legitimate social standing."

"I understand that, but surely—"

"You do not understand." He cut across her protest with sharp authority. "A spinster lady of eight-and-twenty, travelling about unaccompanied, asking pointed questions about deceased gentlemen's private papers? Such behaviour would occasion precisely the sort of gossip you hope to avoid. Within a week, half of London would be speculating about your activities."

The casual reference to her age and unmarried state brought fresh heat to her cheeks, but she forced herself to focus on his meaning rather than his manner. "Then what do you suggest?"

Edward rose from his chair and began to pace before the fireplace, his hands clasped behind his back. "I suggest we provide you with social protection. A reason for your sudden interest in investigation that will appear entirely natural and proper."

"What sort of reason?"

He turned to face her directly, and she was struck by the calculating intelligence in those pale blue eyes. "An engagement, Miss Hartwell. A betrothal to a gentleman of sufficient standing to make your presence in society unremarkable."

Poppy stared at him in bewilderment. "I beg your pardon, but I am not engaged to anyone."

"No, but you could be. Temporarily."

The implications of his words struck her like a physical blow. "You're suggesting... that is, you cannot mean..."

"I am suggesting that you and I announce a false engagement," he said with maddening calm. "It would provide the perfect explanation for your sudden appearance in my life and give us both freedom to move about society as an acknowledged couple. No one questions the activities of an engaged pair, particularly when they are seen to be taking an interest in their mutual social connections."

Poppy felt the room spinning slightly around her. "Mr Taverner, that is... that would be..." She struggled to find words adequate to express her shock. "It would be a complete deception!"

"Yes," he agreed cheerfully. "A most useful one."

"It would be dishonest!"

"Undoubtedly."

"It would be..." She cast about for a more compelling argument. "It would be scandalous if the truth were discovered!"

"Less scandalous than whatever secrets your father's papers might contain, I suspect." His tone grew more serious. "Miss Hartwell, I understand your reservations, but consider the alternatives. You can return to London, pay whatever sum your blackmailer demands, and hope that proves sufficient to purchase his permanent silence. Or you can fight back with the only weapons available to us—deception and misdirection."

Poppy rose from her chair and moved to the window, staring out at the gathering dusk. The prospect of deliberate dishonesty went against every principle of proper behaviour she had been taught. Ladies did not engage in elaborate deceptions. They did not form false alliances with disreputable gentlemen. They certainly did not announce fictitious engagements for purposes of social manipulation.

And yet...

"How would such an arrangement work?" she heard herself asking.

"Simply enough. We would announce our engagement through the usual channels—a notice in the papers, letters to key social figures. I would escort you to various functions where we might encounter people who knew your father. As an engaged couple, we would be expected to discuss our future together, our families' histories, our shared interests. Such conversations would provide ample opportunity to gather information."

"But your reputation," Poppy protested, turning back to face him. "Mr Pemberton told me of your... difficulties. Would not an association with you damage my standing rather than protect it?"

Edward's expression darkened. "My fall from grace was spectacular but brief, Miss Hartwell. The legal profession has a short memory for such scandals, particularly when newer ones arise to capture attention. And while I may no longer practice law, I retain my family name and connections. The Taverner title may be in abeyance, but it still carries weight in certain circles."

"What would be expected of me? In terms of... behaviour?"

"Nothing improper, I assure you. We would

appear together at social functions, conduct ourselves as any engaged couple might, and gradually extract the information we require. Once your blackmailer is identified and dealt with, we would discover some irreconcilable difference of opinion and quietly dissolve the engagement. Such things happen frequently enough to occasion little comment."

The fire settled in the grate with a soft crash of burning logs, sending up a shower of sparks. Poppy watched them rise and disappear into the chimney, feeling as though her own carefully ordered life were similarly dissolving into smoke and uncertainty.

"There would need to be rules," she said finally. "Clear boundaries regarding what would and would not be acceptable."

"Naturally."

"And a definite end point. I will not be party to an indefinite deception."

"Agreed. Shall we say three months? If we have not resolved the matter by then, we dissolve the arrangement regardless."

"And absolute discretion. No one else must know the truth."

"Of course." Edward moved to stand before her,

extending his hand formally. "Do we have an agreement, Miss Hartwell?"

Poppy stared at his outstretched hand, knowing that taking it would commit her to a course of action that would have horrified her mere days ago. But the memory of her mother's fragile health and Rose's glowing happiness strengthened her resolve.

"We do," she said, placing her hand briefly in his.

His fingers were warm despite the chill of the room, and she felt an odd jolt of sensation at the contact. This was the hand that would soon wear her ring, she realized with a start. The hand that would escort her through London's drawing rooms as they played out their elaborate charade.

"Excellent." Edward released her hand and moved back to his chair. "Now, we must discuss the practical details. When did we meet? How did our attachment develop? What are our plans for the future?"

"Surely such details are unnecessary..."

"On the contrary, they are essential. Any engaged couple would be expected to share such information freely. If our stories contradict each other, we shall be exposed immediately."

For the next hour, they worked through the framework of their fictional romance with the methodical precision of generals planning a military campaign. They had met, they decided, through mutual friends during Poppy's recent visit to the countryside. Their attachment had developed through correspondence, and Edward had recently proposed during a romantic walk through the gardens at Taverner Hall.

"What about the ring?" Poppy asked suddenly. "Surely I would be expected to wear an engagement ring?"

Edward's expression grew thoughtful. "Yes, that is a consideration. There are family pieces, of course, though most are..." He gestured vaguely at their surroundings. "Let us say they are currently being cleaned and reset. You shall receive the ring within the week."

As they concluded their planning, the sound of a door opening echoed through the hall, followed by footsteps on the stone floor. Lady Agnes appeared in the doorway, carrying a tea tray.

"I thought you might require refreshment," she said, her dark eyes moving between them with keen interest. "You've been closeted together for quite some time."

"Miss Hartwell and I have been discussing business," Edward replied smoothly. "She has agreed to assist me with a legal matter of some delicacy."

"How... convenient." Lady Agnes set the tray down with perhaps more force than was strictly necessary. "And will this assistance require Miss Hartwell to remain at Taverner Hall for an extended period?"

"Actually," Edward said, glancing at Poppy, "Miss Hartwell has just done me the honour of accepting my proposal of marriage."

The teacup Lady Agnes was holding slipped from her fingers, shattering on the stone hearth with a sound like breaking crystal. The silence that followed seemed to stretch for an eternity, broken only by the crackling of the fire and the soft tick of the mantel clock.

"Indeed," Lady Agnes said finally, her voice carrying an undertone that made Poppy's skin crawl. "How... sudden."

"Sometimes," Edward replied, his tone deliberately casual, "the heart knows its own mind with remarkable clarity."

Lady Agnes bent to collect the broken china, her movements sharp and precise. "Of course. How foolish of me to be surprised. After all, it has been so long since Taverner Hall welcomed a... happy event."

There was something in the way she spoke the words that suggested happiness was the last thing she associated with the crumbling estate. As she straightened, her eyes fixed on Poppy with an intensity that was almost physical.

"You must be very... courageous, Miss Hartwell, to attach yourself to this family. We have not had the best of luck with such arrangements in recent years."

Before Poppy could ask what she meant, a sharp knock echoed through the hall. Edward frowned, glancing toward the door.

"We are not expecting anyone," Lady Agnes said, her voice tight with what might have been alarm.

The knock came again, more insistent this time. Edward strode from the room, leaving Poppy alone with Lady Agnes, who continued to watch her with those penetrating dark eyes.

"Tell me, Miss Hartwell," the older woman said softly, "do you believe in curses?"

"I... what?"

"Curses. Family curses. The sort of thing that follows bloodlines through generations, striking down the innocent along with the guilty."

The sound of voices drifted from the entrance hall—Edward's deep tones and another man's higher, more nasal voice. Poppy strained to hear what was being said, but the words were indistinct.

"I'm afraid I don't understand," she managed.

"No," Lady Agnes said, her lips curving in what might have been a smile. "I don't suppose you do. But you will, my dear. You will."

The library door opened to admit Edward, his expression grim. Behind him stood a thin, nervous-looking man in clerk's clothing, clutching a leather satchel.

"Miss Hartwell," Edward said, his voice carefully controlled, "it appears we have received word from your blackmailer. Mr Crowhurst here has delivered a message that requires your immediate attention."

The man stepped forward, offering a sealed envelope with shaking hands. "Begging your pardon, miss, but I was told to deliver this personally and wait for a response."

Poppy's heart hammered against her ribs as she accepted the letter. The paper was of the same quality as the first message, and her name was written in the same careful script. But as she broke the seal and unfolded the contents, she felt the blood drain from her face.

Miss Hartwell,

Your recent activities have not gone unnoticed. Travel-

ling to Norfolk to consult with disgraced persons will not resolve your difficulties—indeed, such actions only demonstrate how desperately you require guidance.

You have one week to reconsider your position. The sum required for my continued discretion is £500, to be delivered according to instructions I shall provide.

Any further attempts at investigation will result in immediate publication of your father's most damaging revelations.

Your servant in this matter,

A Concerned Party

The letter trembled in Poppy's hands as the full implications struck her. Not only had her blackmailer learned of her visit to Taverner Hall, but the price of silence had finally been given. Five hundred pounds was a fortune—more than her family's annual income from their remaining investments.

"Well?" Edward asked quietly.

Poppy looked up at him, then at Lady Agnes, who was watching the proceedings with obvious fascination. The nervous clerk continued to hover near the door, clearly expecting some form of response.

"He wants five hundred pounds," she said, her voice barely above a whisper. "And he knows I came here."

Edward's jaw tightened. "Then it appears our

arrangement has become more urgent than anticipated. Mr Crowhurst, you may tell your employer
that Miss Hartwell requires time to consider his
proposal. She will contact him within the week."

The clerk nodded rapidly and backed toward the
door. "Yes, sir. I'll tell him exactly that, sir."

As soon as he was gone, Edward turned to Poppy
with an expression of grim determination.

"It seems, Miss Hartwell, that we are no longer
merely planning a deception. We are embarking
upon a war."

CHAPTER 5

The morning of their first public appearance dawned crisp and clear, with autumn sunlight streaming through the tall windows of Belmont House. Poppy stood before her looking glass, adjusting the emerald brooch at her throat for the third time, her hands trembling slightly with nervous energy.

The engagement ring Edward had sent lay in its velvet box on her dressing table—a delicate band of gold set with a modest sapphire surrounded by tiny diamonds. It was beautiful in its simplicity, and when she had slipped it onto her finger the previous evening, she had been surprised by how natural it felt there. Now, as she prepared to wear it in public for the first time, the weight of it seemed enormous.

"You look lovely, dear," her mother said from the doorway, though her voice carried a note of puzzlement. "I must confess, I'm still rather shocked by your news. To think you've been conducting a secret correspondence all this time, and we never suspected a thing."

Poppy's cheeks burned with the familiar guilt of deception. The story she and Edward had agreed upon—a gradual courtship conducted through letters after a chance meeting in the countryside—had been accepted by her family with varying degrees of surprise and delight. Rose had been rapturous, immediately launching into plans for a double wedding, while their mother had been more cautious, expressing concern about the haste of the attachment.

"Sometimes these things develop quite naturally, Mama," Poppy replied, turning away from the mirror. "Mr Taverner and I found we had much in common."

"Yes, so you've said. Though I do wish we had met the gentleman before the engagement was announced. It would have been more... conventional."

The word hung in the air between them, a gentle rebuke that made Poppy's conscience writhe. Her entire life had been built upon convention, upon doing what was proper and expected. Now she found herself enmeshed in a web of lies that grew more complex with each passing hour.

"He will be calling this afternoon," she said. "You'll have ample opportunity to form your own opinion of him then."

Lady Catherine nodded, though her expression remained troubled. "I hope he proves worthy of you, my dear. You've sacrificed so much for our family's welfare these past years. You deserve happiness."

The irony of these words was not lost on Poppy. She was indeed sacrificing for her family's welfare, but in ways her mother could never imagine. As for happiness... that seemed a luxury she could ill afford at present.

The sound of carriage wheels on the gravel drive announced Edward's arrival precisely at the appointed hour. Poppy watched from the drawing room window as he descended from a hired conveyance, noting how different he appeared in London dress. Gone was the country gentleman in worn clothes; in his place stood a figure of undeniable elegance, his dark coat perfectly fitted, his bearing that of a man accustomed to moving in the highest circles.

Jenkins announced him with the formal courtesy due to a family connection, and Poppy felt her pulse quicken as Edward entered the room. For a moment, their eyes met across the space between them, and she saw something flicker in his pale gaze—perhaps amusement, perhaps something else entirely.

"Mr Taverner," she said, rising gracefully. "How punctual you are."

"I would never keep my intended waiting," he replied, taking her hand and raising it briefly to his lips. The gesture was perfectly proper, yet something in the way his fingers lingered on hers made her breath catch.

Rose bounced to her feet with barely contained excitement. "Oh, how romantic! Poppy, you never told us how handsome he is!"

Edward's lips curved in what might have been genuine amusement. "Miss Rose, I believe? Your sister has told me so much about you."

"All good things, I hope," Rose said with a giggle. "Though I must scold you terribly for stealing her away so suddenly. We had quite given up hope of her ever marrying, you know."

"Rose!" Poppy's cheeks flamed with embarrassment.

"What? It's perfectly true. You're nearly thirty,

after all, and we'd all assumed you were destined for spinsterhood. Not that there's anything wrong with that, of course, but—"

"I think," Lady Catherine interrupted firmly, "we should allow Mr Taverner to settle himself before subjecting him to an inquisition."

As they took tea together, Poppy watched her family's reaction to Edward with growing fascination. He was, she had to admit, playing his role to perfection. With Rose, he was indulgent and mildly teasing, drawing her out about her own upcoming wedding with just the right degree of brotherly interest. With Lady Catherine, he was respectful and deferential, speaking knowledgeably about topics that would interest a woman of her generation and social standing.

"I understand you've been living rather quietly in Norfolk," Lady Catherine said, offering him a second cup of tea. "That must have been quite an adjustment after your legal career."

Poppy held her breath, wondering how he would navigate this delicate territory. The story of his disgrace was not entirely secret, and her mother was far too intelligent to be completely ignorant of his history.

"Indeed it was," Edward replied smoothly. "But I

found the peace of the countryside conducive to... reflection. Sometimes a man must step back from the world to understand his place in it."

"Very philosophical," Lady Catherine murmured, though her tone suggested she was not entirely convinced.

When the time came to depart for Lady Pemberton's afternoon salon, Poppy felt as though she were preparing for battle. This would be their first public appearance as an engaged couple, their first test before the scrutinizing eyes of London society.

"You look pale," Edward observed quietly as he handed her into his carriage. "Having second thoughts?"

"Merely nervous," she replied, settling her skirts around her. "I've never been particularly adept at deception."

"Then it's fortunate that the best deceptions contain elements of truth. We are indeed working together toward a common goal. We do have reasons to spend time in each other's company. The engagement is simply... a convenient framework for these activities."

His practical approach to their situation should have been reassuring, but instead, it reminded her of how completely artificial their arrangement was. She was an actress playing a role, nothing more.

Lady Pemberton's salon occupied the ground floor of her elegant Mayfair mansion, where society's most influential ladies gathered weekly to discuss literature, politics, and—most importantly— gossip. As they were announced and made their entrance, Poppy felt the weight of dozens of curious gazes upon them.

"Miss Hartwell," Lady Pemberton exclaimed, gliding forward with obvious delight. "And this must be the mysterious Mr Taverner we've all been so eager to meet."

"Lady Pemberton," Edward said, bowing over her hand with practiced grace. "Your reputation for hospitality precedes you."

"Flatterer," she replied with evident pleasure. "Come, you must tell us everything. Such a romantic tale—a secret correspondence, a proposal in a moonlit garden. It's quite like something from a novel."

As they were swept into the gathering, Poppy found herself separated from Edward by the press of eager ladies, each demanding details about their courtship. She answered as best she could, sticking to the story they had rehearsed, but the constant scrutiny left her feeling exposed and vulnerable.

"My dear," Mrs Aldrich said, taking her arm confidentially, "you must tell me honestly—is it true what they say about Mr Taverner's... difficulties? That business with the Redmayne case?"

Poppy's heart stumbled. The name meant nothing to her, but Mrs Aldrich's tone suggested it should. "I'm afraid I don't know what you mean," she replied carefully.

"Oh, surely you must have heard. The scandal was quite the thing several years ago. Mr Taverner was defending some railway speculator—Redmayne, I think his name was—who was accused of the most dreadful financial irregularities. The case collapsed quite dramatically when evidence went missing, and there were suggestions that Mr Taverner himself might have been... well, that he might not have been entirely ethical in his methods."

The room seemed to spin slightly around Poppy. She had known Edward's career had ended in scandal, but the specific details had remained vague. Now, faced with this casual revelation, she felt the ground shifting beneath her feet.

"I'm sure there were misunderstandings," she managed to say.

"Oh, I'm certain you're right," Mrs Aldrich replied with the sort of smile that suggested she was certain of no such thing. "Still, one does wonder why a gentleman of his background would choose to bury himself in the countryside for so long. Not that it matters now, of course. Love conquers all, as they say."

Across the room, Edward was engaged in animated conversation with several gentlemen, his manner easy and confident. Whatever shadows might hang over his past, he showed no sign of being troubled by them in present company.

As the afternoon wore on, Poppy found herself increasingly uncomfortable with the role she was playing. Every compliment on her engagement felt like a rebuke, every expression of congratulation like a weight upon her conscience. When Lady Pemberton called for attention and proposed a toast to the happy couple, Poppy thought she might actually faint from the combined pressure of guilt and anxiety.

"To Miss Hartwell and Mr Taverner," Lady Pemberton declared, raising her teacup in lieu of a proper glass. "May their union be blessed with every happiness."

The assembled ladies echoed the sentiment, and

Poppy forced herself to smile and nod graciously while inside she felt like a fraud of the worst sort. These women had shown her nothing but kindness over the years, and she was repaying that kindness with elaborate deception.

It was only when they were finally in the carriage returning to Belmont House that she allowed herself to truly breathe. The performance was over, at least for now.

"You did well," Edward said, settling back against the leather seats. "Lady Pemberton was quite charmed, and I heard several invitations being extended for future engagements."

"Mrs Aldrich mentioned something called the Redmayne case," Poppy said without preamble. "She seemed to think it was significant."

Edward's expression darkened. "Did she indeed? How obliging of her to bring up ancient history."

"Is it ancient history, Mr Taverner? Or is it something I should know about, given our... arrangement?"

For a long moment, he said nothing, staring out at the London streets passing by their window. When he finally spoke, his voice was carefully controlled.

"Lord Redmayne was a man of considerable

influence who found himself accused of defrauding investors in a railway scheme. I was engaged to defend him, and I believed him to be innocent. During the course of my investigation, I uncovered evidence that suggested the real culprit was someone far more powerful—someone with connections throughout the government and legal establishment."

"What happened?"

"The evidence disappeared. Key witnesses recanted their testimony. My own reputation was systematically destroyed through a campaign of whispers and innuendo. Lord Redmayne was quietly acquitted, and I was left to bear the blame for the entire affair."

Poppy studied his profile, noting the tension in his jaw. "Do you believe Lord Redmayne was truly innocent?"

"I believe," Edward said slowly, "that justice was not served. And I believe that the forces which destroyed my career are still very much at work in London society."

A chill ran down Poppy's spine that had nothing to do with the autumn air. "Are you suggesting that my father's blackmailer might be connected to these same forces?"

"I'm suggesting that men of power protect their secrets by any means necessary. If your father's journals contain information that could threaten such men..." He turned to meet her gaze directly. "Then we may be facing enemies far more dangerous than a simple blackmailer seeking financial gain."

The carriage had stopped before Belmont House, but neither of them moved to alight. The weight of Edward's revelation settled over Poppy like a suffocating blanket.

"The five hundred pounds," she said quietly. "It's not really about the money, is it?"

"No," Edward replied. "I suspect it's about ensuring that whatever is in your father's journals never sees the light of day."

As they sat there in the gathering dusk, Poppy felt the last of her illusions about their situation crumble away. She had thought herself dealing with a common criminal, someone motivated by greed and opportunity. Instead, she might be facing the same powerful forces that had destroyed Edward's career and driven him into exile.

"What do we do now?" she asked.

"Now," Edward said, his voice carrying a note of grim determination, "we return to Norfolk and begin searching for those journals in earnest.

Because I suspect that finding them is the only way to discover who our true enemy is."

"And the blackmailer's deadline?"

"We ignore it. Let him make his threats. If we're right about the nature of this conspiracy, he won't risk exposing the journals' contents any more than we will. The question is whether we can find them before he decides we've become too dangerous to leave alive."

The words hung in the air between them like a physical presence. Poppy stared at her engagement ring, its modest sapphire catching the last rays of sunlight through the carriage window. What had begun as a simple matter of family protection had transformed into something far more sinister.

But there was no turning back now. She was committed to this path, for better or worse.

When she finally spoke, her voice was steady despite the fear coursing through her veins.

"Very well then, Mr Taverner. Let us return to Norfolk and begin the real hunt."

CHAPTER 6

The return journey to Taverner Hall took place under leaden skies that seemed to mirror Poppy's increasingly troubled state of mind. As the hired carriage rolled through the Norfolk countryside, she found herself starting at every unexpected sound—the cry of a crow, the creak of the vehicle's springs, the driver's occasional calls to his horses. The coded passage she had discovered in her father's journal lay safely tucked within her reticule, but its cryptic symbols seemed to burn through the leather like a brand.

She'd felt so uncomfortable with the idea of reading her father's journal. It had felt like a betrayal, an invasion, but she settled herself with the knowledge that somewhere out there someone knew something about her father that she didn't. Something that could cause chaos in her family. Something that she needed to know.

When she'd finally opened up the journal, it's contents had been surprisingly bland. No more than the day to day appointments that he'd kept, but at the back of the journal, tucked into the last few pages, she'd discovered something. Passages of writing written in some kind of code. Poppy was certain that they were important.

Edward sat opposite her in contemplative silence, his pale eyes fixed on the passing landscape. He had said little since they had left London.

Now, as Taverner Hall's Gothic towers came into view through the autumn mist, Poppy felt a curious mixture of dread and relief. The crumbling estate might be unwelcoming, but at least here they could speak freely without fear of being overheard by curious servants or nosy neighbours.

The carriage drew to a halt before the imposing entrance, and Edward handed her down with the sort of careful courtesy that had become second nature during their brief engagement charade. As they approached the great door, it swung open to reveal Lady Agnes waiting in the shadowed entrance hall.

"So," the older woman said, her dark eyes moving between them with obvious interest, "the happy couple returns. I trust your performance in London was suitably convincing?"

Poppy felt heat rise in her cheeks. "Lady Agnes, I—"

"Oh, my dear child, there's no need for pretence here," Lady Agnes interrupted with a wave of her black-gloved hand. "The walls of Taverner Hall have heard far more shocking deceptions than yours. Haven't they, Edward?"

Something passed between them—a look that spoke of shared secrets and old wounds. Edward's jaw tightened almost imperceptibly before he responded.

"Perhaps we might postpone the philosophical discussions until after Miss Hartwell has had an opportunity to refresh herself," he said coolly. "The journey was rather trying."

"Of course." Lady Agnes inclined her head graciously. "Mrs Fletcher has prepared the Blue Room for Miss Hartwell's use. I do hope you'll find it comfortable, my dear. It has such... interesting associations."

As they climbed the main staircase, Poppy couldn't shake the feeling that Lady Agnes's words carried some deeper meaning. The Blue Room, when they reached it, proved to be a reasonably comfortable chamber despite the general decay that plagued the rest of the house. The walls were panelled in faded silk the colour of winter sky, and tall windows looked out over what had once been formal gardens but now ran wild with brambles and untended roses.

"The room is perfectly lovely," Poppy said, setting down her travelling case.

"It was my brother Sebastian's favourite," Edward replied, his tone carefully neutral. "He spent many hours here during his final illness."

Another piece of the Taverner family puzzle, though one that raised more questions than it answered. Poppy was beginning to understand that Taverner Hall was layered with secrets like an ancient manuscript, each generation adding its own sorrows to the palimpsest of family history.

That evening, as they gathered in the library after a simple dinner, the true work began. Edward had cleared a space on the massive oak table, and by the light of several oil lamps, they spread out the coded journal pages alongside sheets of fresh paper for their attempts at decryption.

"The most common approach to such ciphers,"

Edward explained, taking up a pen, "is to look for patterns that might correspond to frequently used words or letters. If your father was writing in English, certain combinations will appear more often than others."

Poppy watched, fascinated despite her anxiety, as he began to mark the repeated symbol groups with different colours. His hands moved with the precise efficiency of a man accustomed to working with complex documents, and she found herself oddly distracted by the way the lamplight caught the angular planes of his face.

"Here," he said after perhaps an hour of painstaking work. "This three-symbol combination appears seven times in just this one page. In English text of this length, I would expect to see 'the' approximately that often."

"So those symbols represent T-H-E?"

"Possibly. Let me see if that assumption leads to other recognizable patterns."

As the evening wore on, they worked in companionable concentration, the only sounds the scratch of pen on paper and the occasional hiss and pop from the fireplace. Lady Agnes appeared periodically with offers of tea or brandy, her presence a silent reminder that they were not entirely alone with their secrets.

It was past ten o'clock when Edward suddenly straightened, his pale eyes bright with discovery.

"I believe I have it," he said, his voice tight with excitement. "Look here—if we assume this symbol represents 'R' and this one 'E', then this phrase becomes 'REDMAYNE PAPERS HIDDEN'."

Poppy's breath caught. "Redmayne? The same man from your legal case?"

"The very same." Edward's expression had grown grim. "It appears your father knew more about Lord Redmayne's affairs than anyone suspected."

Before Poppy could respond, a sound from else-where in the house made them both freeze. It was subtle—perhaps no more than a floorboard settling —but in the profound quiet of the Norfolk country-side, it seemed unnaturally loud.

"Did you hear that?" Poppy whispered.

Edward was already on his feet, moving silently toward the library door. He pressed his ear against the heavy wood for a moment, then turned back to her with a finger raised to his lips.

The sound came again—definitely footsteps now, slow and deliberate, moving through the corridor beyond. But Lady Agnes had retired to her chambers an hour ago, and the servants had long since finished their evening duties.

Edward eased the door open just wide enough to peer out into the darkened hallway. After a moment, he gestured for Poppy to join him. Through the narrow gap, she could see a faint light moving along the far end of the corridor—not the steady glow of a lamp, but the flickering dance of a candle held by an unseen hand.

"Who could it be?" she breathed.

"I don't know," Edward murmured back. "But we're going to find out."

He opened the door wider and stepped into the corridor, Poppy close behind him. The candlelight had disappeared around a corner, but they could still hear the soft whisper of footsteps on stone. Moving as quietly as possible, they followed the sound deeper into the house, through passages Poppy had never explored.

The footsteps led them to a part of Taverner Hall that seemed even more decrepit than the rest. Here, many of the doors stood ajar, revealing chambers that were clearly no longer in use. Dust sheets covered the furniture like ghostly shrouds, and the air carried the musty scent of long abandonment.

"This is the east wing," Edward explained in a

whisper. "It's been closed for years—since Sebastian's death."

They paused at the entrance to a long gallery lined with portraits of long-dead Taverners. The candlelight had vanished, but they could hear movement from somewhere ahead—the soft sound of a door opening and closing.

"We should go back," Poppy whispered, suddenly acutely aware of how isolated they were in this forgotten part of the house. "If someone is prowling about..."

"If someone is prowling about," Edward replied grimly, "I intend to know who and why."

They pressed on through the gallery, past the stern gazes of Edward's ancestors, until they reached a heavy oak door that stood slightly ajar. Beyond it lay another corridor, this one lined with smaller chambers that might once have housed visiting servants or minor guests.

The sound of voices drifted from one of these rooms—hushed but unmistakably real. Edward approached the partially open door with careful steps, Poppy following despite every instinct that urged her to flee.

Through the gap, they could see into a small sitting room furnished with dust-covered chairs and a single table. Lady Agnes stood in the centre of the space, still dressed in her evening clothes but now holding a candle that cast dancing shadows on the walls around her.

She was not alone.

A man stood with his back to the door, his form partially obscured by the uncertain light. He was speaking in urgent, hushed tones, though the words were too quiet to make out clearly. Lady Agnes listened with the intense concentration of someone receiving vital intelligence.

"...must be found before they decode more..." The man's voice rose just enough for them to catch this fragment.

"I understand the urgency," Lady Agnes replied, her tone sharp with impatience. "But I cannot simply search their belongings without arousing suspicion. The girl is not stupid, whatever else she might be."

Poppy felt Edward tense beside her. They were discussing her—and presumably the coded journal pages now lying on the library table.

"The deadline approaches," the man continued. "If they cannot be persuaded to abandon this investigation..."

"Then we shall have to consider other measures,"

Lady Agnes finished coldly. "I am quite aware of what is at stake."

The conversation continued for several more minutes, but the speakers' voices had dropped too low to be heard clearly. Eventually, the man moved toward what must have been another exit from the room, disappearing into the shadows beyond their limited view.

Lady Agnes remained for a moment longer, staring down at something on the table that they could not see. Then she too departed, taking her candle with her and plunging the chamber into darkness.

Edward and Poppy remained frozen in place for several minutes, hardly daring to breathe. Only when they were certain Lady Agnes had truly gone did they begin the careful journey back to the library.

"She knows," Poppy whispered once they were safely behind the library door. "She knows about the journals, about what we're trying to do."

"More than that," Edward replied, his voice tight with anger and something that might have been pain. "She's actively working against us. That man— whoever he was—they're coordinating their efforts to stop our investigation."

Poppy sank into her chair, feeling as though the ground had shifted beneath her feet. "But why? What possible interest could Lady Agnes have in protecting Lord Redmayne?"

Edward moved to the fireplace, staring into the dying embers. "I don't know," he said finally. "But I suspect it has something to do with Sebastian's death. Agnes has always been... secretive about the circumstances of my brother's final illness."

"You think there's a connection?"

"I think," Edward said slowly, "that this house holds more secrets than either of us realized. And I think we may be in considerably more danger than we first understood."

The coded journal pages still lay spread across the table, their partial decryption revealing tantalizing glimpses of the truth. But now those symbols seemed less like a puzzle to be solved and more like a map leading into increasingly treacherous territory.

"What do we do now?" Poppy asked.

Edward turned from the fireplace, his pale eyes hard with determination. "Now we decode the rest of these passages as quickly as possible. Because I have a feeling that whatever your father discovered about Lord Redmayne is the key to understanding everything—including why my brother died and why someone is so desperate to keep us from learning the truth."

As if summoned by his words, the wind outside picked up, rattling the ancient windows and sending a shower of sparks up the chimney. Somewhere in the depths of Taverner Hall, a door slammed shut with a sound like a gunshot.

Poppy pulled her shawl more tightly around her shoulders and reached for her pen. Whatever secrets this crumbling house contained, whatever dangers they might face, she was committed now to seeing this through to its conclusion.

The game had become far more deadly than either of them had anticipated, but there was no turning back.

CHAPTER 7

The morning after their disturbing discovery brought a grey dawn that seemed to seep through the very stones of Taverner Hall. Poppy had slept poorly, haunted by dreams of shadowy figures moving through corridors and whispered conversations just beyond her comprehension. When she finally descended to the breakfast room, she found Edward already seated at the table, his attention focused on a letter that had arrived with the morning post.

"More correspondence from your admirers in London?" she asked, attempting lightness despite the tension that had settled over them like a pall.

Edward looked up, and she was struck by the weariness in his pale eyes. "A letter from Rose, actually. She writes that the preparations for her wedding continue apace, though she mentions some... concerns among your social circle."

Poppy's heart clenched. "What sort of concerns?"

"Nothing specific, merely whispers and speculation. It seems our engagement has provoked more interest than we anticipated." He folded the letter carefully and set it aside. "She also mentions that your mother has been asking pointed questions about my family's circumstances."

The guilt that had become Poppy's constant companion twisted more sharply in her chest. "I should return to London. My prolonged absence is causing exactly the sort of talk we hoped to avoid."

"Perhaps. But first, we must finish decoding your father's papers. What we discovered last night about Redmayne's connection to your family suggests the danger is more immediate than we realized."

They worked together in the library through the morning hours, the coded symbols gradually yielding their secrets under Edward's methodical approach. As each line was translated, the scope of her father's knowledge became increasingly clear—and increasingly damning.

"Look at this passage," Edward said, his voice tight with controlled excitement. "'Redmayne inheritance fraudulent—documents forged—beneficiary unaware.' Your father wasn't simply aware of Lord Redmayne's crimes, Poppy. He had evidence of them."

"Forged inheritance documents?" Poppy leaned closer to study the translation, her shoulder brushing against Edward's. The contact sent an unexpected flutter through her, and she found herself distracted by the warmth radiating from him despite the morning chill. "What could that mean?"

"It could mean that Lord Redmayne's entire fortune—his title, his estates, his position in society —all of it might be built on fraudulent claims." Edward's hands stilled on the papers, and when he looked at her, she was startled by the intensity in his gaze. "Do you understand what that would mean? The scandal would destroy not just Redmayne, but potentially dozens of others who have benefited from their association with him."

The implications were staggering, but Poppy found herself oddly distracted by how close they were sitting, by the way the morning light caught the silver threads in Edward's dark hair. When had she begun to notice such details? When had the angular planes of his face become so familiar, so... compelling?

"Poppy?" His voice was soft, questioning, and she realized she had been staring.

"I... yes, I understand," she said quickly, pulling back and pretending to study the papers with renewed interest. "No wonder someone is so desperate to suppress this information."

But even as she spoke, she was acutely aware of Edward's continued presence beside her, of the way he unconsciously leaned toward her when pointing out particularly significant passages. Their false engagement had required them to play the part of an attached couple in public, but here, in the privacy of Taverner Hall's library, there should have been no need for such proximity.

Yet neither of them seemed inclined to move away.

"There's more," Edward said, his voice dropping to barely above a whisper. "This section here—it mentions witnesses to the forgery. Names, dates, specific details that could corroborate the accusations."

"Where are these witnesses now?"

"That," Edward replied grimly, "is an excellent question. If they're still alive, they represent the final proof needed to bring down Redmayne and his entire network. If they're not..."

He didn't need to finish the thought. They both understood that men like Redmayne didn't hesitate to eliminate threats to their power and position.

The sound of the library door opening made them spring apart like guilty conspirators. Lady Agnes entered carrying a tea tray, her dark eyes moving between them with obvious interest.

"How dedicated you both are to your... research," she said, setting the tray down with perhaps more force than necessary. "I do hope you're making progress."

"Some," Edward replied carefully. "Though we're finding the material more complex than anticipated."

"Complex." Lady Agnes repeated the word as though tasting something unpleasant. "Yes, I imagine it would be. The past has a way of becoming quite tangled, doesn't it? Particularly when it involves matters that were meant to remain buried."

There was something in her tone that made Poppy's skin crawl—a subtle threat wrapped in polite conversation. After the previous night's revelations, every word from Lady Agnes seemed laden with hidden meaning.

"Some things," Poppy said carefully, "deserve to be brought to light, regardless of how deeply they've been buried."

Lady Agnes smiled, but there was no warmth in the expression. "How idealistic of you, my dear. Though I wonder if you've considered the cost of such... illumination. Truth can be a dangerous thing, particularly for those unprepared to face its consequences."

The older woman glided from the room as silently as she had entered, leaving behind only the faint scent of lavender and an atmosphere of barely concealed menace.

"She knows," Poppy said as soon as they were alone again. "She knows exactly what we've discovered."

"More than that," Edward replied, his expression troubled. "I think she's trying to warn us off. The question is whether that warning comes from concern for our welfare or fear for her own secrets."

They returned to their work, but the easy companionship of the morning had been shattered. Every sound from the corridor beyond made them tense, every shadow seemed potentially threatening. When the afternoon post arrived with another letter, this one bearing Rose's familiar handwriting, Poppy almost welcomed the distraction.

But her relief was short-lived.

"Oh no," she breathed, scanning the contents rapidly. "Edward, we have a problem."

"What is it?"

"Rose writes that James has been asking questions about your background. Apparently, some of his friends have been spreading stories about the Redmayne case, suggesting that your involvement was more... questionable than you've admitted."

Edward's face went very still. "What sort of stories?"

"She doesn't provide details, but she says James is concerned about the potential impact on his own reputation. He's... he's suggested that perhaps Rose should reconsider her association with our family until the matter is resolved."

The words hung in the air between them like a poison cloud. If James Whitmore withdrew his offer of marriage, Rose would be ruined. No other gentleman of his standing would risk association with a family touched by scandal.

"I should never have involved you in this," Edward said, rising abruptly from his chair. "I should have realized that my reputation would taint anyone associated with me."

"Don't be ridiculous," Poppy replied, though her

heart was racing. "We entered into this arrangement with full knowledge of the risks."

"Did we?" Edward turned to face her, and she was shocked by the pain in his pale eyes. "Did you truly understand what it would mean to attach your name to mine? To risk everything your family has worked for these past years?"

Something in his tone—a vulnerability she had never heard before—made her step closer without conscious thought. "Edward, we can find a way through this. We simply need to—"

"To what? Continue this charade until your sister's reputation is destroyed along with my own? Until your mother's health fails under the strain of fresh scandal?" He ran a hand through his hair, a gesture that spoke of deep frustration. "Perhaps it would be better if we dissolved our arrangement now, before any more damage is done."

"No." The word came out more forcefully than Poppy had intended. "No, we cannot give up now. We're too close to the truth."

"The truth." Edward laughed bitterly. "The truth is that I'm a broken man living in a crumbling house, surviving on the remnants of a fortune destroyed by my own arrogance. The truth is that I should never have presumed to involve someone like you in my battles against the forces that ruined my life."

"Someone like me?" Poppy felt heat rise in her cheeks. "What exactly do you mean by that?"

"I mean someone decent. Someone honourable. Someone who deserves better than to be dragged down by association with my failures."

The pain in his voice was raw, unguarded, and it struck something deep within Poppy's chest. Without thinking, she reached out and caught his hand in hers.

"Edward, stop. You're not a failure. What happened to you wasn't your fault—it was the result of corruption and conspiracy by men who feared the truth you were trying to expose."

He stared down at their joined hands, his expression unreadable. "You don't understand what I've done. What I've lost. What I've cost my family."

"Then tell me," she said simply. "Tell me about Sebastian."

The name fell between them like a stone into still water, sending ripples of emotion across Edward's features. For a moment, she thought he would refuse to answer. Then, slowly, he began to speak.

"Sebastian was three years younger than I, but he was everything I should have been. Brilliant, charming, genuinely good in ways I never managed to be. He should have inherited the title, the estate, the responsibility. Instead, he inherited the consequences of my disgrace."

Edward moved to the window, still holding her hand, drawing her with him to look out at the wild gardens beyond.

"When the Redmayne case collapsed and my career was destroyed, Sebastian stood by me. He refused to believe the accusations, defended me to anyone who would listen. But the scandal touched him too—invitations stopped coming, friends turned away, his own prospects began to crumble."

"That's not your fault," Poppy said softly.

"Isn't it?" Edward's grip on her hand tightened. "He began drinking heavily, became reckless, desperate to restore the family's reputation. He invested what remained of our fortune in increasingly risky ventures, always chasing the one opportunity that would set everything right. And when those investments failed..."

He trailed off, but Poppy could see the rest of the story written in the lines of grief around his eyes.

"He took his own life," she said, the words barely a whisper.

"The official cause was a riding accident. Sebastian was an excellent horseman, but he'd been drinking, and the horse threw him. Whether it was truly an accident or..." Edward shrugged helplessly. "Agnes blames me, and she's right to do so. If I hadn't been so determined to fight Redmayne, to expose corruption I couldn't prove, Sebastian would still be alive."

They stood in silence for several moments, looking out at the testament to the Taverner family's decline. Poppy felt her heart breaking for this man who carried such an impossible burden of guilt and responsibility.

"You couldn't have known," she said finally. "You were fighting for justice, for truth. Those are noble goals, even when they lead to tragedy."

"Are they worth your sister's happiness? Your family's reputation?" Edward turned to face her fully, and she was struck by how close they were standing, by the intensity in his pale eyes. "Because that's what we're risking, Poppy. Every day we continue this investigation, we risk destroying everything you hold dear."

She should step back, should put proper distance between them. Instead, she found herself moving closer, drawn by something she couldn't name.

"Some things," she said, her voice barely audible, "are worth the risk."

For a moment, the world seemed to narrow to just the two of them—to the space between their bodies, to the way Edward's eyes darkened as he looked down at her, to the sudden, overwhelming awareness of him as a man rather than simply an ally in their dangerous game.

Then his hand rose to cup her cheek, and she felt her breath catch in her throat.

"Poppy," he said, her name a question and a plea all at once.

She should pull away. Should remember that their engagement was a fiction, their partnership a matter of necessity rather than choice. Should think of her family, her reputation, her duty to behave as a proper young lady.

Instead, she leaned into his touch and whispered, "Yes."

When his lips met hers, it was with a gentleness that seemed to acknowledge the fragility of the moment. This was not the calculated gesture of their public performance, but something real and precious and infinitely more dangerous.

The kiss lasted only seconds, but when they broke apart, Poppy felt as though something fundamental had shifted between them. Edward's hand remained on her cheek, his thumb tracing a gentle path along her cheekbone.

"I should apologize," he said, though he made no move to step away.

"Should you?" Poppy asked, surprised by her own boldness. "Because I find I'm not at all sorry it happened."

Something flickered in Edward's eyes—surprise, perhaps, or hope. But before he could respond, the library door burst open and Lady Agnes swept in, her face flushed with obvious agitation.

"Edward, we have visitors," she announced, her gaze moving suspiciously between them. "Three gentlemen from London. They claim to be conducting some sort of official inquiry, and they're asking very pointed questions about Miss Hartwell's presence here."

The spell of the moment shattered completely. Edward stepped back from Poppy, his expression hardening into the mask of polite indifference she had come to know so well.

"Official inquiry?" he repeated. "On whose authority?"

"They carry papers bearing Lord Redmayne's seal," Lady Agnes replied, her voice heavy with meaning. "It appears, my dear nephew, that your past has finally caught up with you."

As the implications of this announcement settled over them, Poppy felt the fragile happiness of the past few minutes crumble into dust. Whatever understanding she and Edward had just reached, whatever feelings had begun to bloom between them, would have to wait.

Their enemies had found them, and the real battle was about to begin.

CHAPTER 8

The three gentlemen waiting in Taverner Hall's drawing room had the unmistakable bearing of men accustomed to wielding authority. Their dark coats and stern expressions gave them the appearance of carrion birds, and Poppy felt a chill of apprehension as Edward led her into their presence.

"Mr Taverner," the eldest of the three said, rising with calculated courtesy. "I am Mr Bradshaw, representing certain interested parties in London. These are my associates, Mr Henley and Mr Price."

Edward's manner was coolly polite as he acknowledged the introductions, but Poppy could see the tension in the rigid line of his shoulders.

"Gentlemen. To what do I owe this unexpected visit?"

"We understand you are currently engaged to Miss Hartwell," Mr Bradshaw continued, his pale eyes fixing on Poppy with uncomfortable intensity. "A young lady whose late father left behind certain... documents that have attracted unwanted attention."

"I'm not sure I follow your meaning," Edward replied, though his voice carried a warning edge.

"Come now, Mr Taverner. We need not play games with one another." Mr Bradshaw moved to the window, gazing out at the unkempt gardens with obvious distaste. "Sir Charles Hartwell kept detailed journals during his parliamentary career. Journals that contain speculation and accusations that certain parties would prefer to remain private."

Poppy felt her heart begin to race, but she forced herself to maintain an expression of polite confusion. "I'm afraid I don't understand what my father's private papers could possibly have to do with—"

"Miss Hartwell," Mr Henley interrupted, his voice carrying a note of barely concealed menace, "we know you have been attempting to decode these journals. We know you have discovered references to matters that are... sensitive in nature."

The game was up, then. Somehow, these men

knew exactly what she and Edward had been doing. The thought of Lady Agnes's midnight conversation filled Poppy's mind, but she pushed it aside. There would be time for recriminations later.

"Suppose, for the sake of argument," Edward said carefully, "that such journals existed and contained the information you suggest. What concern would that be of yours?"

Mr Bradshaw turned from the window, his expression hardening. "The concern, Mr Taverner, is that irresponsible speculation about respected members of society serves no one's interests. Least of all those of Miss Hartwell and her family."

"Are you threatening us?" Poppy asked, surprised by her own boldness.

"Not at all," Mr Price spoke for the first time, his voice smooth as silk. "We are merely offering... guidance. You see, Miss Hartwell, your sister's engagement to Mr Whitmore hangs by the slenderest of threads. Your mother's health is already fragile. It would be tragic if unnecessary scandal were to cause further deterioration in either situation."

The casual cruelty of the threat took Poppy's breath away. These men knew exactly where to strike to cause the maximum damage to her family.

"What do you want?" she asked quietly.

"Simply for you to cease this fruitless investigation," Mr Bradshaw replied. "Return to London, marry Mr Taverner if you wish, and allow the past to remain buried where it belongs."

"And if we refuse?"

Mr Henley smiled, but there was no warmth in the expression. "Then I fear the consequences would be most unpleasant for all concerned."

After the three men had departed with their veiled threats still hanging in the air, Poppy and Edward retreated to the library in grim silence. The coded journal pages lay scattered across the table exactly as they had left them, but their innocent appearance now seemed mocking.

"They knew too much," Edward said finally, settling into his chair with obvious weariness. "Not just about the journals' existence, but about our progress in decoding them."

"Lady Agnes," Poppy replied flatly. "It has to be. She's been reporting our activities to someone."

"Perhaps. Or perhaps they have other sources of information." Edward picked up one of the translated pages, studying it with renewed intensity. "But if they're this desperate to stop us, it means we're close to something truly damaging."

"Close to what, though? We know your father

suspected Redmayne of forgery, but we still don't know the specific details."

Edward was silent for a long moment, his pale eyes scanning the symbols that had yielded only partial secrets. Then, suddenly, he straightened.

"Poppy, look at this passage again. This section here that we thought was corrupted—what if it's not code at all, but rather abbreviations?"

She leaned closer, following his pointing finger. "You mean like legal shorthand?"

"Exactly. Your father was trained in law before entering Parliament. He would have been familiar with the standard abbreviations used in legal documents." Edward's voice was growing excited as he worked through the implications. "If we apply those conventions to this section..."

He began writing rapidly, translating the cryptic symbols using legal terminology rather than the substitution cipher they had been assuming. As the words took shape on the paper, Poppy felt her breath catch.

"'Redmayne inheritance documents examined,'" she read aloud. "'Original will of Seventh Earl discovered in Chancery archives. Current claimant illegitimate—true heir unknown.'"

"There's more," Edward said, his pen moving

frantically across the page. "Forged papers witnessed by Thompson, clerk to Mr Aldridge of Gray's Inn. Original documents hidden—location known to myself alone.'"

The magnitude of what they were reading slowly sank in. If her father was correct, then Lord Redmayne had built his entire position in society on fraudulent claims to a title and estate that rightfully belonged to someone else.

"Thompson," Poppy repeated. "That's one of the witnesses my father mentioned. If he's still alive—"

"Then we have corroboration for the accusations," Edward finished. "But first, we need to find those original documents."

"My father says the location is known to him alone. Where would he have hidden such dangerous evidence?"

Edward studied the translated text again, his brow furrowed in concentration. "Here, at the end—there's another abbreviation. 'S.D.B.' followed by what looks like a number sequence."

"Safe deposit box," Poppy said immediately. "Father had an account at Rothschild's Bank. He always said their security was beyond reproach."

"Then that's where we'll find the proof we need." Edward gathered the papers together with quick, efficient movements. "We leave for London at first light."

"Edward, wait." Poppy caught his hand, stilling his frantic activity. "Those men made it very clear what would happen if we continued this investigation. Are we prepared for the consequences?"

He looked down at their joined hands, and she was reminded of the kiss they had shared just hours earlier. So much had changed since then—not just their circumstances, but something fundamental between them.

"I won't lie to you, Poppy. The danger is real, and it's growing. Redmayne and his associates have already demonstrated their willingness to destroy anyone who threatens their secrets. If we proceed, we'll be putting not just ourselves at risk, but your entire family."

"But if we don't proceed, they win. The truth remains buried, and men like Redmayne continue to profit from their crimes."

"Yes." Edward's voice was quiet but firm. "That's exactly what it means."

She thought of Rose, radiant in her wedding preparations, trusting that her sister would never do anything to jeopardize her happiness. She thought of her mother, already weakened by years of worry and grief, who could not survive another scandal. And she thought of her father, who had died carrying these terrible secrets, believing perhaps that they would die with him.

"We have to try," she said finally. "We have to at least find the documents and see what evidence really exists. We owe that much to everyone who's been hurt by Redmayne's deception."

Edward raised their joined hands to his lips, pressing a gentle kiss to her knuckles. "Then we face whatever comes together."

The words carried weight beyond their immediate meaning. Whatever happened in the coming days, whatever dangers they might encounter, they would meet them as true partners rather than mere allies of convenience.

As evening fell over Taverner Hall, they made their preparations for the journey to London. Edward armed himself with a pistol that had belonged to his brother, while Poppy packed the translated journal pages in a secure compartment of her traveling case.

Lady Agnes appeared as they were making their final arrangements, her dark eyes taking in their obvious preparations for departure.

"Leaving so soon?" she asked, her voice carrying

that familiar undertone of menace. "I do hope your business in London proves... successful."

"I'm sure it will," Edward replied evenly. "Thank you for your hospitality, Agnes."

"Think nothing of it. After all, family must support one another through difficult times." Her gaze fixed on Poppy with uncomfortable intensity. "I do hope, Miss Hartwell, that you understand the risks you're taking. Not just for yourself, but for those you claim to love."

"I understand them perfectly," Poppy replied, meeting the older woman's stare without flinching.

"Do you? How... admirable." Lady Agnes moved toward the door, then paused. "I wonder if you've considered what you'll do if the truth proves to be more devastating than the lies you're so eager to expose."

With that cryptic warning, she glided from the room, leaving Poppy with the uncomfortable feeling that there were still secrets within secrets that she had yet to uncover.

That night, as she lay in the Blue Room listening to the wind howl around the towers of Taverner Hall, Poppy found sleep elusive. Tomorrow would bring them back to London and potentially to the evidence that could destroy Lord Redmayne. But it would also bring them face to face with enemies who had already proven their willingness to use any means necessary to protect their interests.

Somewhere in the darkness of the hall, she heard footsteps—slow, deliberate, moving through corridors that should have been empty. But this time, she made no move to investigate. Whatever shadows haunted Taverner Hall, she and Edward would soon be beyond their reach.

The real question was whether they would be walking into something far worse in London.

As dawn approached, Poppy rose and dressed carefully for the journey. When she descended to the entrance hall, she found Edward waiting with their luggage and a hired carriage. His face was grim but determined, and when he handed her into the vehicle, his touch lingered just a moment longer than strictly necessary.

"Are you ready for this?" he asked quietly.

Poppy looked back at Taverner Hall one last time, its Gothic towers dark against the grey morning sky. Somewhere within those crumbling walls lay the answers to questions about Sebastian's death and Lady Agnes's true loyalties. But those mysteries would have to wait.

"I'm ready," she said, and meant it.

As the carriage rolled away from the estate, carrying them toward whatever awaited in London, Poppy felt a strange mixture of fear and anticipation. They were no longer simply investigating a blackmail scheme or protecting her family's reputation. They were about to challenge some of the most powerful men in England, armed with nothing but a dead man's journals and their own determination to see justice done.

The game had become far more dangerous than either of them had anticipated, but there was no turning back now. Redmayne's reach was vast, his influence widespread, but he had made one crucial error.

He had underestimated the power of truth to destroy even the most carefully constructed lies.

CHAPTER 9

*T*he journey back to London passed in tense silence, both Poppy and Edward lost in their own thoughts as the Norfolk countryside gave way to the sprawling outskirts of the capital. It was only as their carriage approached the familiar streets of Mayfair that Edward finally spoke.

"We should go to your family's house first," he said, his voice carefully neutral. "There are arrangements to be made before we can safely approach Rothschild's Bank."

Poppy nodded, though her stomach churned with anxiety at the thought of facing her mother and Rose while carrying such dangerous secrets. The weight of the decoded journal pages in her traveling case seemed to grow heavier with each passing mile.

When they arrived at Belmont House, Jenkins greeted them with obvious relief, though his weathered face showed signs of strain.

"Miss Hartwell, Mr Taverner," he said, accepting their coats with practiced efficiency. "I'm afraid there have been... developments in your absence."

"What sort of developments?" Poppy asked, her heart immediately leaping to thoughts of her family's welfare.

"Perhaps it would be best if you spoke with Lady Catherine directly," Jenkins replied diplomatically. "She is in the morning room with Miss Rose."

They found Lady Catherine and Rose huddled together on the settee, their faces bearing expressions of obvious distress. Rose's eyes were red-rimmed with recent tears, while their mother appeared more fragile than Poppy had ever seen her.

"Poppy!" Rose leaped to her feet and rushed into her sister's arms. "Oh, thank goodness you're back. Everything has been perfectly dreadful."

"What's happened?" Poppy asked, stroking her sister's hair while exchanging a worried glance with Edward over Rose's head.

"It's James," Rose sobbed against her shoulder.

"He's broken our engagement. He says his family cannot be associated with scandal, and that questions about Mr Taverner's past make it impossible for him to proceed with our marriage."

The words hit Poppy like a physical blow. This was exactly what they had feared, exactly what Redmayne's men had threatened. Her investigation had cost Rose her chance at happiness and security.

"I'm so sorry," she whispered, tightening her embrace. "Rose, I'm so terribly sorry."

"It's not your fault," Rose said, pulling back to wipe her eyes. "You couldn't have known that pursuing your own happiness would cause such difficulties."

If only it were that simple, Poppy thought with bitter irony. If only she were truly engaged to Edward for reasons of love rather than necessity.

Lady Catherine rose from the settee with obvious effort, moving to take Edward's hands in hers. "Mr Taverner, I hope you will not take offense, but I must ask—are the allegations against you true? Did you truly engage in unethical conduct during that legal case?"

Edward's face went very still, and Poppy held her breath, waiting to see how he would respond. So much depended on his answer, not just for their investigation but for any hope of salvaging her family's reputation.

"Lady Catherine," he said quietly, "I give you my word as a gentleman that I have never acted dishonourably in my professional capacity. The accusations against me were orchestrated by powerful men who feared the truth I was attempting to expose."

"Then why did you not fight to clear your name?"

"Because the forces arrayed against me were too powerful, and I lacked the evidence needed to prove their corruption. Fighting would have only prolonged the scandal and potentially endangered others." His eyes found Poppy's across the room. "I chose exile over a battle I could not win."

Lady Catherine studied his face intently, then nodded slowly. "I believe you, Mr Taverner. And I want you to know that this family stands by you, regardless of what society may whisper."

The simple dignity of her mother's declaration brought tears to Poppy's eyes. Here was proof, if any were needed, of why the fight for truth was worth the risks they were taking.

"There is something else," Rose said hesitantly. "A young girl arrived this morning asking to speak with you, Poppy. She said it was a matter of the utmost urgency."

"A young girl?" Poppy frowned. "What was her name?"

"Lucy Taverner," Rose replied, glancing at Edward. "She said she was Mr Taverner's niece."

Edward went very pale. "Lucy? But that's impossible. She's at school in Bath."

"She's waiting in the small sitting room," Lady Catherine said. "Jenkins thought it best not to turn her away, given her connection to the family."

They found Lucy Taverner in the sitting room, perched on the edge of a chair like a bird ready to take flight. She was perhaps sixteen years old, with Edward's distinctive pale eyes and an air of barely contained energy that spoke of intelligence and determination.

"Uncle Edward!" She leaped to her feet as they entered, rushing to embrace him with obvious relief. "Thank goodness you're here. I've been so worried."

"Lucy, what are you doing in London? You should be at school."

"I had to come," she said, her young face serious beyond her years. "There are things happening— dangerous things—and I couldn't just sit in Bath pretending ignorance."

Edward's expression grew stern. "What sort of things?"

Lucy glanced around the room, her gaze settling on Poppy with obvious curiosity. "Is this Miss Hartwell? The lady you're engaged to?"

"Yes," Edward replied carefully. "Lucy, this is Miss Poppy Hartwell. Poppy, my brother's daughter, Lucy."

"I'm pleased to meet you," Poppy said, offering her hand. "Though I confess I'm confused about why you're here."

Lucy shook her hand briefly, then turned back to Edward with obvious urgency. "Uncle, there have been men asking questions at school. Gentlemen from London who wanted to know about our family, about you specifically. They offered money to any of the girls who could provide information about your activities."

A chill ran down Poppy's spine. Redmayne's reach extended even to a young ladies' academy in Bath.

"What did you tell them?" Edward asked.

"Nothing, of course. But some of the other girls... well, they thought it was terribly exciting. They told these men about the letters you've been receiving, about how you seemed more animated lately than you had in years." Lucy's voice dropped to a whisper. "Uncle, I think they're planning something terrible."

"What makes you say that?"

"Because I overheard them talking to Miss Smythe, the headmistress. They suggested that perhaps it would be safer if I didn't return to school after the holidays. They said there were concerns about my family's... stability."

The implication was clear. They were moving to isolate Lucy, to remove her from any position where she might provide information or support to Edward's cause.

"You did right to come here," Edward said, placing a protective hand on his niece's shoulder. "But Lucy, I need you to understand—the situation is more dangerous than you realize."

"I don't care about danger," Lucy replied with the fearless conviction of youth. "I care about family. Father would have wanted me to stand by you, just as you always stood by him."

The mention of Sebastian brought a shadow of pain across Edward's features, but also something that might have been pride.

"Very well," he said finally. "But you must promise to follow my instructions exactly. No heroics, no independent action. Can you do that?"

"I promise."

As they discussed arrangements for Lucy's

accommodation, Poppy found herself studying the girl with growing interest. There was something about her—an intelligence and determination that reminded her of Edward himself—that suggested she might prove to be more than just another person to protect.

"Lucy," she said suddenly, "you mentioned that men were asking questions at your school. Did you happen to notice anything about them? Their appearance, their manner of speaking?"

"Oh, yes," Lucy replied eagerly. "One of them had a peculiar scar across his left hand, shaped rather like a crescent moon. And he spoke with what I thought might be an Irish accent, though he was trying to disguise it."

Edward and Poppy exchanged glances. This level of detail could prove useful in identifying their enemies.

"There's something else," Lucy continued. "At Christmas, when I was home at Taverner Hall, I found Aunt Agnes going through Father's old papers. When I asked her what she was looking for, she became quite agitated and told me to mind my own affairs. But I saw some of the documents— they had official seals and looked terribly important."

"What kind of seals?" Poppy asked, her heart beginning to race.

"Government seals, I think. And one that looked like it might belong to a bank or legal firm."

The pieces of the puzzle were beginning to fall into place. Lady Agnes hadn't merely been reporting their activities to Redmayne's agents—she had been actively searching for evidence that could be used against them.

"Lucy," Edward said seriously, "I need you to think very carefully. Did you see any names on those documents? Anything that might help us understand what Aunt Agnes was looking for?"

Lucy screwed up her face in concentration. "There was one name I recognized—Redmayne. I remembered it because of all the talk about your legal case. But there were others too... Whitmore was one, I think."

"Whitmore?" Rose spoke for the first time since they'd entered the room. "But that's James's family name."

The silence that followed this revelation was deafening. If the Whitmore family was somehow connected to Redmayne's network, then James's sudden withdrawal from their engagement took on a much more sinister meaning.

"We need to get to that bank," Edward said grimly. "Whatever evidence your father left there, it's becoming clear that multiple parties are desperate to either find it or ensure it remains hidden."

"But Uncle," Lucy interjected, "surely you're not thinking of going alone? These men are clearly dangerous, and if they've been watching you..."

"We'll be careful," Poppy assured her, though she herself was beginning to feel the weight of the forces arrayed against them.

"No," Lucy said firmly, rising from her chair with an expression of determination that was pure Taverner. "You'll need help. Someone they wouldn't expect, someone who could watch for trouble while you conduct your business."

"Absolutely not," Edward replied immediately. "Lucy, I will not put you in danger."

"Uncle, you're not putting me in danger—I'm already in danger simply by being your niece. But I could be useful. These men are looking for a couple, not a family party. A young lady accompanying her uncle and his fiancée on a banking errand would appear perfectly innocent."

Despite her youth, Lucy's logic was sound. And as Poppy looked at the girl's determined face, she felt a flicker of something she hadn't experienced in days —hope.

"She has a point," Poppy said quietly. "And we could use all the allies we can find."

Edward looked between them, his expression torn between protectiveness and practicality. Finally, he sighed in defeat.

"Very well. But at the first sign of trouble, you leave immediately. No arguments, no heroics. Agreed?"

"Agreed," Lucy said, though her eyes sparkled with excitement that suggested she might not be entirely truthful about avoiding heroics.

As they made their final preparations for the visit to Rothschild's Bank, Poppy felt the dynamics of their mission shifting once again. What had begun as her solitary struggle against a blackmailer had evolved into something much larger—a battle for truth that now involved not just herself and Edward, but his brave young niece as well.

The dangers were multiplying, but so was their determination. Whatever evidence lay waiting in that safe deposit box, whatever secrets her father had died protecting, they would uncover them together.

The forces of corruption might be powerful, but

they had made one crucial error. They had underestimated the strength that came from family loyalty and the willingness of good people to stand together against injustice.

As Lucy chattered excitedly about their plans, bringing new life to the household that had been shrouded in gloom, Poppy allowed herself a moment of cautious optimism. Perhaps they really could win this fight after all.

CHAPTER 10

The morning dawned grey and misty, perfectly matching Poppy's apprehensive mood as she prepared for their expedition to Rothschild's Bank. She had spent a restless night thinking about the revelations concerning the Whitmore family's possible connection to Lord Redmayne, and the implications of what they might discover in her father's safe deposit box.

Lucy proved to be an early riser, appearing in the breakfast room before even Edward had descended. The young woman was dressed in a sensible dark blue walking dress, her pale hair neatly arranged beneath a modest bonnet that suggested a proper young lady on a routine outing with her family.

"I've been thinking about our strategy," she

announced without preamble, settling herself at the table with the confidence of someone accustomed to being heard. "If these men are watching for Uncle Edward and Miss Hartwell together, we should vary our approach to the bank."

"What do you suggest?" Poppy asked, impressed despite herself by Lucy's tactical thinking.

"Well, Uncle Edward should arrive first, perhaps ten minutes before us. He can conduct his business while we remain outside, watching for any suspicious activity. If anything seems amiss, I can create a distraction while you both make your escape."

Edward entered the breakfast room in time to hear this last suggestion, and his expression immediately darkened. "Lucy, we discussed this. You are not to put yourself in danger."

"I wouldn't be in danger," Lucy replied with the sort of logic that only the young could muster. "I would simply be a schoolgirl who had become separated from her companions and was asking for directions. Perfectly innocent."

"There is nothing innocent about any aspect of this situation," Edward said firmly, though Poppy caught a note of reluctant admiration in his voice. "These are not men who would hesitate to harm anyone they perceived as a threat, regardless of age or gender."

"All the more reason for us to be clever about how we approach this," Lucy countered. "Uncle, you've been fighting these people for years, and where has direct confrontation gotten you? Perhaps it's time to try a different approach."

The conversation was interrupted by the arrival of Jenkins, who approached with his usual discretion but obvious urgency.

"Forgive the intrusion," he said quietly, "but there are men watching the house. They've been positioned across the square since dawn, and they show no signs of departing."

Poppy felt her stomach clench with anxiety. "How many men?"

"Two that I can see clearly, miss. There may be others positioned where they're less visible."

Edward moved to the window, carefully positioning himself where he could observe without being seen. After a moment, he returned to the table, his expression grim.

"Redmayne is moving more quickly than we anticipated," he said. "They're not even bothering to maintain the pretence of subtlety anymore."

"Then we can't simply walk out the front door

and proceed to the bank as planned," Poppy observed.

"No, we cannot." Edward began pacing, his mind clearly working through alternatives. "We need another way out of the house, and we need to approach our destination by an indirect route."

"The service entrance," Lucy suggested immediately. "Surely your servants come and go without attracting attention?"

Jenkins cleared his throat delicately. "Indeed, miss. The tradesmen's entrance opens onto the mews, which connects to three different streets. It would be quite possible to depart unobserved, particularly if one were dressed appropriately."

The idea of disguising themselves as servants would have been scandalous under normal circumstances, but these were far from normal circumstances. Poppy found herself nodding slowly.

"It could work," she said. "But we would need to be very careful about timing."

"Leave that to me," Jenkins said with quiet confidence. "I have been managing the comings and goings of this household for twenty years. I believe I can arrange for a suitable distraction."

As they refined their plans, Poppy couldn't help but marvel at how their desperate situation was bringing out unexpected qualities in everyone involved. Jenkins was revealing strategic talents that went far beyond his duties as a butler, while Lucy was proving to have a mind that was both tactical and fearless.

"There's something else we need to consider," Edward said as they finalized the details. "Even if we successfully reach the bank and retrieve whatever evidence your father left there, we need to have a plan for what comes next."

"What do you mean?" Poppy asked.

"I mean that simply possessing proof of Redmayne's crimes won't be enough. We need to ensure that evidence reaches people who have both the power and the will to act upon it. And we need to do so before Redmayne's associates can silence us permanently."

The stark reality of their situation settled over the breakfast room like a chill. They weren't simply trying to solve a mystery or clear Edward's name— they were engaged in a race against time where the stakes were their very lives.

"I have an idea about that," Lucy said quietly. "There's a journalist who has been writing about political corruption for The Times. My schoolmistress mentioned him because she believes young ladies should be aware of current affairs. Mr Jonathan Hartley—he's made quite a reputation exposing scandals among the powerful."

"A reformist journalist," Edward mused. "That could work, provided we can reach him safely."

"More than that," Lucy continued with growing excitement, "he's known for protecting his sources. If we can get the evidence to him, he would ensure it reaches the proper authorities while keeping us anonymous."

It was a solid plan, though one that would require them to survive long enough to implement it. As the morning progressed, they made their final preparations with the meticulous care of generals planning a campaign.

Poppy found herself alone with Edward for a few moments while Lucy was upstairs changing into more suitable attire for their deception.

"Edward," she said softly, "I need you to know that whatever happens today, I don't regret our partnership. Even if it costs my family everything, I believe we're doing the right thing."

He turned from where he had been studying a map of London's banking district, his pale eyes intense with emotion she was learning to recognize.

"Poppy, there's something I need to tell you

before we proceed further," he said, moving closer. "When this began, our engagement was nothing more than a convenient fiction. But somewhere along the way..."

He paused, seeming to struggle with words that had never come easily to him.

"What I'm trying to say is that my feelings for you have become entirely real. Whatever danger we face today, whatever happens in the coming days, I want you to know that I love you. Truly and completely."

The words she had longed to hear and feared to hope for hung in the air between them. Poppy felt her heart racing, not with anxiety this time, but with a joy so intense it was almost painful.

"Edward," she whispered, reaching out to touch his face. "I love you too. I think I have for weeks, though I was afraid to admit it even to myself."

He caught her hand in his, pressing it against his cheek. "Then whatever comes, we face it together. Not as partners in a deception, but as two people who have found something worth fighting for."

Before she could respond, he leaned down and kissed her with a passion that spoke of all the emotions they had been forced to suppress. This was not the careful, calculated gesture of their public performance, but something desperate and genuine and full of promise.

When they broke apart, both breathing heavily, Lucy's voice drifted down from upstairs.

"Uncle Edward! Miss Hartwell! I believe it's time we departed if we're to maintain our schedule!"

The spell of the moment was broken, but the understanding between them remained. Whatever happened at Rothschild's Bank, whatever revelations awaited in her father's safe deposit box, they would face it as partners in every sense of the word.

"Are you ready for this?" Edward asked, his voice husky with emotion.

"I'm ready," Poppy replied, and meant it.

They made their way to the service entrance, where Jenkins had assembled a collection of servants' clothing that would serve as their disguises. Lucy appeared dressed as a kitchen maid, her aristocratic bearing carefully concealed beneath a mobcap and apron. Edward would pose as a tradesman making deliveries, while Poppy would be his assistant.

"Remember," Jenkins said as he surveyed their transformation, "move confidently but not conspicuously. Servants who act nervous draw attention."

"And if we're discovered?" Lucy asked.

"Then you run," Edward said firmly. "No heroics, no attempts to fight. You get away and warn the others."

As they prepared to leave through the mews, Poppy took one last look at the home that had sheltered her family for so many years. By evening, they would either have the evidence needed to destroy Lord Redmayne's network of corruption, or they would be fugitives running for their lives.

"Second thoughts?" Edward asked quietly.

"No," Poppy replied, adjusting the plain shawl around her shoulders. "Only determination."

Lucy grinned at them both, her young face bright with excitement despite the danger they faced. "Then let's go change the world."

As they stepped out into the London morning, Poppy felt a strange mixture of fear and exhilaration. The game they had been playing was about to reach its climax, and everything they had worked toward hung in the balance.

But they were no longer alone in their fight. They had each other, and Lucy's fierce loyalty, and the quiet support of servants like Jenkins who understood that sometimes justice required ordinary people to do extraordinary things.

The forces of corruption might be powerful, but

they had underestimated the strength that came from love and determination and the willingness to sacrifice everything for the truth.

Whatever waited for them at Rothschild's Bank, they would face it together.

CHAPTER 11

The disguise proved more effective than Poppy had dared hope. Dressed as servants and moving through London's back streets, they attracted no attention from the well-dressed gentlemen who had been watching Belmont House. By mid-morning, they had successfully reached the imposing facade of Rothschild's Bank on New Court, though not without incident.

Twice during their circuitous journey, Lucy had spotted men who seemed to be searching the crowds with particular intensity. Her quick thinking had guided them through side streets and market squares, always staying one step ahead of their pursuers.

"There," Edward said quietly as they positioned

themselves across from the bank's entrance. "The gentleman in the grey coat—I believe that's Mr Aldridge, the contact my former colleague arranged."

Poppy studied the man in question. He appeared to be in his fifties, with the sort of nervous energy that suggested someone unaccustomed to clandestine meetings. He kept checking his pocket watch and glancing around the street with obvious anxiety.

"He looks terrified," Lucy observed with the frank assessment of youth.

"He has reason to be," Edward replied grimly. "If Redmayne's people discover he's meeting with us, his career—and possibly his life—could be forfeit."

As they watched, Mr Aldridge approached the bank's entrance, paused to speak briefly with one of the uniformed attendants, then disappeared inside. This was their signal to proceed.

"Remember the plan," Edward said as they prepared to cross the street. "Lucy, you remain outside and watch for any sign of trouble. If anything seems amiss—"

"I create a distraction and we all meet at the rendezvous point," Lucy finished. "Uncle, I do listen when you give instructions."

The interior of Rothschild's Bank was a temple to British financial power, all marble columns and gilt fixtures designed to inspire confidence in the institution's permanence. Poppy felt distinctly out of place in her servant's costume, but the clerks paid them no attention as Edward approached the inquiries desk.

"I need to access safe deposit box number 247," he said, producing the key they had found among her father's effects along with the authorization letter Poppy had carefully forged using her father's signature.

The clerk examined the documents with practiced efficiency, then gestured toward a corridor lined with private consulting rooms. "Mr Aldridge is waiting in Room 3, sir. He has the materials you requested."

Poppy's heart raced as they were led down the corridor. Everything they had worked toward, all the danger they had faced, was about to reach its culmination.

Mr Aldridge proved to be exactly as nervous as he had appeared from a distance. He rose hastily as they entered, his hands trembling slightly as he gestured toward a leather portfolio on the table.

"Mr Taverner, I presume? And this must be Miss Hartwell." His voice carried the educated accent of a gentleman, but it was strained with obvious fear. "I must tell you, this is highly irregular. Highly irregular indeed."

"We appreciate the risk you're taking," Edward replied, settling into one of the chairs around the small table. "What can you tell us about the documents?"

Mr Aldridge glanced nervously at the door, then opened the portfolio with shaking hands. "Your father was most... methodical, Miss Hartwell. He brought these materials to the bank some six months before his death, along with specific instructions about their release."

Inside the portfolio lay a collection of documents that made Poppy's breath catch. Original wills, property deeds, and what appeared to be correspondence in Lord Redmayne's own hand—evidence that could destroy the man's entire empire of lies.

"The inheritance fraud was even more extensive than we suspected," Mr Aldridge continued, his voice dropping to barely above a whisper. "Lord Redmayne is not merely claiming a title he doesn't deserve—he's been systematically looting the estate that rightfully belongs to another."

"Who is the true heir?" Poppy asked, studying a document that appeared to be a genealogical chart in her father's careful handwriting.

"That's... complicated." Mr Aldridge pulled out a sheet of paper covered in notes. "The legitimate claimant appears to be a young woman named Miss Catherine Ashford. She's currently living in reduced circumstances, completely unaware of her true heritage."

Before Edward could respond, a commotion from the corridor outside made them all freeze. Raised voices, the sound of rapid footsteps, and then Lady Agnes's unmistakable tones cutting through the noise.

"I assure you, gentlemen, they are here. Mr Taverner would never leave London without first consulting his family's financial arrangements."

Edward was on his feet instantly, gathering the documents with swift efficiency. "The window," he said quietly. "There's a service alley behind the building."

But even as they moved toward their escape route, the door to their consulting room burst open. Lady Agnes stood in the doorway, flanked by the same three men who had visited Taverner Hall. Her dark eyes blazed with what might have been triumph.

"Really, Edward," she said with cold satisfaction,

"did you think you could continue this charade indefinitely?"

"Agnes," Edward replied, his voice carefully controlled despite the desperate circumstances. "I should have known you were behind this."

"Behind it?" Lady Agnes laughed, but there was no humour in the sound. "My dear nephew, I am not behind anything. I am simply trying to prevent you from destroying what remains of our family's reputation."

"By conspiring with the men who killed Sebastian?"

The accusation hung in the air like a physical presence. Lady Agnes went very still, her face draining of colour.

"You know nothing about Sebastian's death," she said finally, her voice barely steady.

"I know more than you think." Edward stepped protectively in front of Poppy, though she could see the tension in every line of his body. "I know that Sebastian discovered something about Redmayne's network. I know that his 'accident' was anything but accidental. And I know that you've been protecting his killers."

"You understand nothing!" Lady Agnes's composure cracked completely, her voice rising to near hysteria. "Everything I have done, every compromise I have made, has been to protect this family from complete destruction!"

The raw pain in her voice was unmistakable, and Poppy felt an unexpected stab of sympathy for the older woman despite her betrayal.

"Then help us now," she said, stepping forward despite Edward's protective gesture. "Lady Agnes, help us bring Sebastian's killers to justice."

For a moment, something flickered in Lady Agnes's eyes—hope, perhaps, or the memory of better times. Then her expression hardened again.

"It's too late for justice," she said flatly. "Sebastian is dead, and nothing we do now will bring him back. But these documents..." She gestured toward the portfolio. "These documents will destroy innocent people along with the guilty."

"What innocent people?" Edward demanded.

Before Lady Agnes could answer, Mr Bradshaw stepped forward, his presence filling the small room with menace.

"This touching family reunion is most illuminating," he said with cold satisfaction, "but I'm afraid it must come to an end. Miss Hartwell, you will surrender those documents immediately."

"I think not," Edward replied, his hand moving

subtly toward his coat where Poppy knew he carried his brother's pistol.

"Oh, but I think you will." Mr Bradshaw smiled, and the expression was genuinely chilling. "You see, we have taken the precaution of securing your charming niece. Young Miss Lucy is currently in our custody, and her continued well-being depends entirely on your cooperation."

The world seemed to tilt around Poppy. Lucy— brave, intelligent Lucy who had insisted on helping them—was now in the hands of these ruthless men.

"You're lying," Edward said, but she could hear the uncertainty in his voice.

"Am I?" Mr Bradshaw produced a small piece of fabric—a fragment of blue wool that could have come from Lucy's dress. "She put up quite a fight, I'm told. Most spirited. But youth is no match for experience, I'm afraid."

Mr Aldridge, who had been cowering in his chair throughout this exchange, suddenly spoke up.

"The documents," he said in a voice that shook with fear. "Perhaps... perhaps we could arrange some sort of compromise? Something that would satisfy all parties?"

"Mr Aldridge," Edward said quietly, "I think you should leave. Now."

But the elderly clerk was already gathering his things, his face pale with terror. "I'm sorry," he whispered as he fled toward the door. "I'm so very sorry."

As soon as he was gone, the atmosphere in the room became even more charged. Lady Agnes moved to stand beside Mr Bradshaw, her allegiance now clear despite the obvious conflict in her expression.

"The documents, Mr Taverner," Mr Bradshaw repeated. "Your niece's life depends on your decision."

Poppy watched Edward's face, seeing the terrible calculation taking place behind his pale eyes. Everything they had worked for, all the evidence needed to expose Redmayne's crimes, balanced against the life of an innocent girl who had trusted them to keep her safe.

"If I give you the documents," Edward said slowly, "how do I know you'll release Lucy unharmed?"

"You don't," Mr Bradshaw replied with brutal honesty. "But you do know what will happen to her if you refuse."

The portfolio lay on the table between them, containing years of her father's careful investigation and the proof needed to bring down one of England's most powerful men. But as Poppy looked at Edward's anguished face, she knew that no cause, however just, was worth the life of someone they loved.

"Edward," she said quietly, "give them what they want."

"Poppy, no. Your father died protecting this evidence."

"And Lucy is alive and needs our protection now." She reached for the portfolio, but Edward caught her hand.

"There has to be another way," he said desperately. "There has to be."

Lady Agnes stepped forward, her expression tortured but determined. "There is no other way," she said. "There never was. Some secrets are too dangerous to expose, and some prices are too high to pay."

But even as she spoke, Poppy caught a glimpse of something in the older woman's eyes—a flicker of communication that seemed directed specifically at her.

"You're right, of course," Poppy said carefully, watching Lady Agnes's face. "Some prices are indeed too high."

Lady Agnes nodded almost imperceptibly, and Poppy understood. Whatever game the older woman was playing, whatever secrets she was protecting, there was more happening here than appeared on the surface.

The question was whether they could trust Lady Agnes enough to follow her lead, or whether doing so would only lead them deeper into danger.

As the standoff continued, with Lucy's life hanging in the balance and the fate of their investigation teetering on a knife's edge, Poppy realized that they were about to discover just how far each of them was willing to go to protect the people they loved.

CHAPTER 12

The tension in the small consulting room was so thick it seemed to press against Poppy's chest as she watched Lady Agnes carefully. There had been something in the older woman's expression—a subtle warning that suggested things were not as they appeared.

"Mr Bradshaw," Lady Agnes said suddenly, her voice carrying an authority that made everyone in the room pay attention, "perhaps we should verify that Miss Lucy is indeed secure before proceeding with any... negotiations."

Bradshaw's eyes narrowed slightly. "That is unnecessary, Lady Agnes. You have my word that the girl is safe."

"Your word." Lady Agnes repeated the phrase

with delicate emphasis. "Yes, I'm sure that carries great weight. However, I find myself concerned about the young lady's welfare. After all, she is family."

Something was happening here that Poppy didn't fully understand, but she sensed an undercurrent of conflict between Lady Agnes and Redmayne's men. Edward must have sensed it too, because his posture shifted almost imperceptibly, ready to act if an opportunity presented itself.

"The girl is perfectly safe," Mr Henley interjected impatiently. "She's being held at a secure location until this matter is resolved."

"Which location?" Lady Agnes asked with deceptive mildness.

"That is not your concern," Bradshaw replied sharply.

The exchange revealed what Poppy had begun to suspect—Lady Agnes's loyalties were more complex than they had initially appeared. Whatever her reasons for initially cooperating with Redmayne's network, she was now clearly having second thoughts.

"Actually," Lady Agnes said, moving to stand behind Edward's chair in what appeared to be a casual gesture, "I believe it very much is my concern.

You see, gentlemen, I'm afraid I may have misled you about the extent of my cooperation."

Her hand brushed against Edward's shoulder as she spoke, and Poppy caught the subtle gesture she made—pointing toward the window behind them.

"What do you mean?" Bradshaw's voice had taken on a dangerous edge.

"I mean that while I have been providing you with information about my nephew's activities, I have also been conducting my own investigation into Sebastian's death. And what I discovered has... changed my perspective considerably."

Edward was now fully alert, his body coiled like a spring. Poppy positioned herself closer to the portfolio of documents, ready to grab it if necessary.

"Lady Agnes," Mr Price spoke for the first time, his voice carrying a note of warning, "I would advise you not to complicate an already delicate situation."

"Oh, but it's far too late for that," Lady Agnes replied with a smile that didn't reach her eyes. "You see, I know where Lucy actually is. And it's not where you've told Mr Taverner she is."

The silence that followed this announcement was deafening. Bradshaw's face had gone very still, while his companions exchanged glances that spoke of rapidly changing calculations.

"That's impossible," Henley said finally.

"Is it? Tell me, when was the last time any of you actually saw the girl? This morning? Yesterday?" Lady Agnes's voice carried a note of triumph. "Because I saw her not thirty minutes ago, safely ensconced in St. James's Church under the protection of Father Morrison and a dozen witnesses."

Poppy felt hope flare in her chest. If Lucy was truly safe, then their position was not as desperate as it had seemed.

"You're bluffing," Bradshaw snarled.

"Am I?" Lady Agnes reached into her reticule and produced a small piece of paper. "This is a note from Lucy herself, written in her own hand and witnessed by the good Father. Would you like to verify the handwriting?"

The paper changed hands, and Poppy watched as Bradshaw's expression grew increasingly thunderous. Whatever was written on that note, it clearly confirmed Lady Agnes's claims.

"This changes nothing," he said finally, though his voice lacked its earlier confidence. "We still have other means of ensuring cooperation."

"Such as?" Edward asked, his tone deceptively calm.

"Such as the safety of Miss Hartwell's family.

Your mother and sister are currently at home, are they not? Such a pity if they were to meet with some unfortunate accident."

The threat sent ice through Poppy's veins, but before she could respond, Lady Agnes laughed—a sound that was genuinely amused.

"Oh, my dear Mr Bradshaw, you really haven't been paying attention, have you? Did you think I would expose my hand without ensuring all the pieces were properly positioned?"

"What are you talking about?"

"I'm talking about the fact that Lady Catherine and Miss Rose are currently enjoying the hospitality of the Archbishop of Canterbury himself. It seems His Grace was most concerned when informed about certain threats against a respectable family. The Church tends to take a dim view of intimidation tactics."

Poppy stared at Lady Agnes in amazement. Somehow, the woman had managed to outmanoeuvre Redmayne's entire network while appearing to cooperate with them.

"This is impossible," Price muttered. "How could you have arranged all this without our knowledge?"

"Because you underestimated me," Lady Agnes replied simply. "You saw an old woman, desperate to protect what remained of her family's reputation. You never considered that I might be intelligent enough to play a longer game."

Bradshaw's composure finally cracked completely. "You treacherous—"

"Careful," Edward interrupted, rising from his chair with fluid grace. "The lady is still my Aunt, and I take a dim view of discourtesy toward family."

The atmosphere in the room had shifted dramatically. Where moments before Poppy had felt trapped and desperate, now she sensed opportunity. Lady Agnes had somehow neutralized their enemies' most potent weapons—the threat to Lucy and to her family.

"Now then," Lady Agnes continued with the satisfaction of someone holding all the cards, "I believe we need to discuss terms. But not here, and not with you gentlemen."

"You cannot simply walk away from this," Henley sputtered. "Lord Redmayne will not—"

"Lord Redmayne will do exactly what he has always done when cornered," Lady Agnes cut him off. "He will sacrifice his subordinates to protect himself. I suggest you consider whether your loyalty to him is worth the price you may be asked to pay."

She moved toward the door with regal composure, pausing only to address Edward and Poppy.

"I believe you have what you came for. Perhaps we should adjourn to a more... suitable venue for our discussions."

Edward gathered the portfolio with swift efficiency, and Poppy found herself following Lady Agnes from the room in a daze. The transformation in their circumstances had been so rapid and unexpected that she was struggling to process what had just happened.

As they emerged from the bank onto the crowded London street, Lady Agnes hailed a passing hansom cab with the ease of someone accustomed to command.

"St. James's Church," she instructed the driver as they climbed inside. "And please hurry."

Once they were seated and the cab was moving through London traffic, Poppy finally found her voice.

"Lady Agnes, I don't understand. If you've been protecting Lucy and my family, why did you pretend to cooperate with Redmayne's men?"

"Because," Lady Agnes replied with a weary sigh, "sometimes the only way to defeat an enemy is to let them believe they have won until you're ready to strike back."

"But the midnight meeting we overheard at Taverner Hall," Edward said. "You were clearly coordinating with someone."

"Indeed I was. With Inspector Bradbury of Scotland Yard, who has been investigating Lord Redmayne's activities for the better part of two years. That man you saw was one of his agents, gathering intelligence about the network's operations."

The pieces of the puzzle were finally falling into place, though the picture they revealed was far more complex than Poppy had imagined.

"Sebastian's death," she said quietly. "You've known all along that it wasn't an accident."

Lady Agnes's composure faltered for the first time, her hands clenching in her lap. "Sebastian discovered evidence of massive financial fraud within Redmayne's organization. When he tried to bring it to the authorities, they threatened not just him, but everyone he cared about. He was... he was trying to protect us all when he took those risks that led to his death."

"Why didn't you tell me?" Edward's voice was raw with emotion. "All these years, I've blamed myself for his choices."

"Because I needed you angry," Lady Agnes replied softly. "I needed you focused on your own guilt rather than investigating Sebastian's death. If you had started asking questions too soon, before I had the evidence needed to protect you, they would have killed you too."

The cab was slowing as they approached their destination, but Poppy barely noticed. The revelation of Lady Agnes's true motives cast everything that had happened in a completely different light.

"The blackmail scheme," she said suddenly. "Was that part of your plan too?"

"No, that was an unfortunate complication. When your father's journals were discovered, Redmayne's people saw an opportunity to acquire potentially damaging evidence while also eliminating a threat. I learned of their intentions and tried to warn you away from the investigation, but you proved to be remarkably... persistent."

"So you decided to help us instead?"

"I decided that perhaps it was time to stop protecting everyone from the truth and start using that truth as a weapon." Lady Agnes looked out at the church spire rising before them. "Sebastian died believing that justice was impossible, that men like Redmayne were too powerful to be brought down. I refuse to let his sacrifice be meaningless."

As the cab drew to a halt, Poppy saw a familiar figure emerge from the church entrance. Lucy was indeed safe, her young face bright with excitement as she hurried toward them.

"Uncle Edward! Miss Hartwell!" she called out. "Lady Agnes said you would come here when everything was settled. Did you get the documents? Did everything go according to plan?"

"More or less," Edward replied, catching his niece in a fierce embrace. "Though the plan was rather more complex than we realized."

As they gathered in the quiet sanctuary of the church, surrounded by the evidence of centuries of faith and the promise of sanctuary, Poppy finally allowed herself to believe that they might actually succeed in their seemingly impossible mission.

But even as she savoured the moment of safety and reunion, she knew their work was far from over. They had the evidence needed to expose Redmayne's crimes, and they had escaped his immediate threats, but the man himself remained free and dangerous.

The real battle was just beginning, and they would need every ally they could find if they hoped to see justice done at last.

CHAPTER 13

⚜

*T*he return journey to Taverner Hall took place under cover of darkness, their small party traveling in a hired carriage with curtains drawn and voices kept to hushed whispers. Lady Agnes had insisted they retrieve certain documents from the estate before proceeding with their plans to expose Redmayne, though she had been evasive about exactly what these materials contained.

"There are records Sebastian kept," she explained as the carriage rolled through the Norfolk countryside. "Evidence he gathered about the railway investments that first brought him into contact with Redmayne's network. Combined with your father's journals, they should provide a complete picture of the conspiracy."

Poppy noticed how Edward's hands clenched whenever Sebastian was mentioned, the grief and guilt he carried still raw despite Lady Agnes's revelations about the true circumstances of his brother's death.

"Why didn't Sebastian simply go to the authorities when he first discovered the fraud?" Lucy asked, her young voice cutting through the tension in the carriage.

"Because the fraud involved members of Parliament, judges, even some within Scotland Yard itself," Lady Agnes replied grimly. "Sebastian learned the hard way that corruption reaches into every level of society when the stakes are high enough."

As they approached the familiar Gothic outline of Taverner Hall, Poppy felt a strange mixture of relief and apprehension. The crumbling estate had become both sanctuary and prison during their investigation, and she couldn't shake the feeling that returning there might be a mistake.

"Something's wrong," Edward said suddenly, his voice tight with alarm.

Looking through the carriage window, Poppy could see what had caught his attention. Light flickered in several of the Hall's windows—not the steady glow of oil lamps, but the dancing, irregular illumination of flames.

"Fire," Lucy whispered, her face pale in the darkness.

Edward was already pounding on the carriage roof, shouting instructions to the driver to increase speed. As they drew closer to the estate, the smell of smoke became unmistakable, acrid and sharp in the night air.

The carriage had barely stopped before Edward leaped down, rushing toward the main entrance with obvious desperation. Poppy followed, while Lady Agnes moved with surprising speed for a woman of her years.

"The east wing," Edward called over his shoulder. "The fire's concentrated in the east wing—that's where my study is located."

The implications were immediately clear. If this was not an accident—and given recent events, it almost certainly was not—then someone had deliberately targeted the very location where Edward's papers and legal documents were stored.

They found the household staff in chaos, servants running back and forth with buckets of water while Mrs. Fletcher, the housekeeper, attempted to coordinate the fire-fighting efforts. The fire had indeed started in Edward's study, spreading rapidly through the dry timbers and ancient furnishings of the east wing.

"How did it start?" Edward demanded, catching Mrs. Fletcher by the arm.

"We don't know, sir," the elderly woman replied, her face streaked with soot. "One of the maids smelled smoke around midnight, and by the time we investigated, the study was already ablaze."

"Has anyone been hurt?"

"No injuries so far, sir, but..." Mrs. Fletcher hesitated, glancing toward the burning wing with obvious distress.

"What is it?"

"Miss Lucy, sir. I saw her run inside—said she needed to retrieve something from her room in the Blue Room. We haven't seen her since."

The words hit Edward like a physical blow, as he looked back to where Poppy and Lady Annes stood expecting to see his niece still standing with them.

Lucy was somewhere inside the burning building, trapped in the very section where the flames were spreading most rapidly.

"Which way did she go?" he demanded.

"The servants' stairs, sir, near the back of the east wing."

Edward didn't wait to hear the rest. He was already running toward the building, ignoring the shouts of the servants who tried to stop him. Poppy started after him, but Lady Agnes caught her arm.

"No," the older woman said firmly. "We cannot lose you both."

For several agonizing minutes, they stood watching the flames consume more and more of the east wing while thick smoke poured from the windows. The servants continued their futile battle against the blaze, but it was clear that the fire was beyond their ability to control.

"There!" Poppy cried, pointing toward an upper window where a figure could be seen silhouetted against the orange glow.

It was Lucy, trapped in what had once been the Blue Room. She appeared to be trying to break the window, but the thick glass and iron casements were resisting her efforts. Smoke was beginning to pour from the room behind her.

"Uncle Edward!" Lucy's voice carried across the courtyard, high and desperate. "Help me!"

Edward emerged from the main entrance, his clothes already singed from his journey through the smoke-filled corridors. He looked up at the window where Lucy was trapped, his face contorting with desperate calculation.

"The ladder!" he shouted to the servants. "Get the longest ladder you can find!"

But even as they scrambled to locate equipment that might reach the upper floors, it was clear that time was running out. The flames behind Lucy were growing brighter, and smoke was beginning to obscure the window.

"I'm going in," Edward declared, starting toward the building.

"Sir, you can't!" Mrs. Fletcher protested. "The stairs have collapsed—there's no way to reach the upper floors from inside."

Edward stood in the courtyard, his face illuminated by the growing conflagration, watching helplessly as the young woman he loved like a daughter fought for her life thirty feet above him. The servants had found a ladder, but it was woefully inadequate for the height they needed to reach.

"Lucy!" he called up to her. "Try to break the window! Jump into the courtyard—we'll catch you!"

But the window was too high, the fall too dangerous. Lucy's attempts to break the glass were growing weaker as the smoke thickened around her.

Then, with a sound like thunder, part of the roof collapsed inward. The flames roared higher, and when the smoke cleared enough for them to see, the window where Lucy had been standing was empty.

"No!" Edward's anguished cry echoed across the courtyard as he lunged toward the building, only to be restrained by three of the strongest servants.

"Sir, please!" Mrs. Fletcher sobbed. "She's gone, sir. There's nothing anyone can do now."

For long moments, Edward fought against their restraining hands, his face a mask of grief and rage. When he finally stopped struggling, it was with the terrible stillness of a man whose world had just crumbled around him.

"Let me go," he said quietly, and something in his voice made the servants release their hold.

Edward sank to his knees in the gravel courtyard, staring up at the burning window where Lucy had made her final desperate stand. The flames continued to consume the east wing, destroying not just the physical structure of Taverner Hall but the last connection Edward had to his brother's memory.

Poppy moved to kneel beside him, placing a gentle hand on his shoulder. She could find no words adequate to the moment, no comfort that could ease the devastating loss of someone so young and brave and full of promise.

Lady Agnes stood frozen nearby, her face etched with a grief that seemed to age her by decades. The loss of Lucy was not just a personal tragedy—it was the destruction of the future, the severing of the family line.

As dawn broke over the devastated estate, the fire brigade arrived from the nearest town, their equipment rattling as they rushed to battle what remained of the blaze. But it was far too late to save either the building or the precious life that had been lost within its walls.

The fire continued to burn, consuming the last remnants of the east wing while Edward knelt in the courtyard, broken by a loss that no amount of justice or vengeance could ever repair.

CHAPTER 14

The days following the fire passed in a blur of ash and anguish. Taverner Hall stood like a wounded giant against the Norfolk sky, its blackened east wing a constant reminder of the tragedy that had befallen them. Where once Gothic towers had risen in stately decay, now only broken walls and charred timbers remained, a monument to loss and the terrible price of their pursuit of justice.

Edward had not spoken since Lucy's funeral three days prior. He moved through the remaining habitable portions of the Hall like a ghost himself, his pale eyes empty of the fierce intelligence that had once burned there. Poppy watched him with growing concern, recognizing in his withdrawal the signs of a man consumed by guilt and grief.

"He blames himself," Lady Agnes said quietly as they stood in what remained of the library, sorting through books that had escaped the flames. "Just as he blamed himself for Sebastian's death. The burden of responsibility has always been Edward's greatest weakness and his greatest strength."

"There must be something we can say to him," Poppy replied, setting aside a volume whose pages had been singed but were still readable. "Some way to make him understand that Lucy's death wasn't his fault."

"Understanding and accepting are different things entirely," Lady Agnes observed with the weary wisdom of someone who had carried her own share of guilt. "Edward will need time to find his way back from this darkness, if indeed he ever does."

The practical matters surrounding the tragedy had fallen largely to Poppy and Lady Agnes to manage. The fire brigade's investigation had concluded that the blaze was deliberately set, though they had no leads as to the perpetrator's identity. The local magistrate had expressed his condolences but made it clear that without witnesses or evidence, there was little he could do to pursue the matter.

More troubling still were the whispers that had begun to circulate in the nearby village. Rumours about the Taverner family's cursed legacy, about the strange deaths that seemed to follow in their wake. Some spoke of divine judgment upon a house that had harboured dark secrets for too long.

"They think we brought this upon ourselves," Poppy said, reading aloud from a letter that had arrived that morning. It was from one of Edward's few remaining friends in London, warning that society's opinion was turning increasingly against them.

"Perhaps we did," Lady Agnes replied with bitter honesty. "Perhaps our pursuit of justice has cost more than we ever intended to pay."

The letter continued with news that was equally devastating in its own way. James Whitmore had not only broken his engagement with Rose but had begun spreading rumours about the Hartwell family's connections to scandal and disgrace. Other families were following suit, distancing themselves from anyone associated with the Taverner name.

"Rose writes that she can barely show her face in society," Poppy continued, her voice heavy with guilt. "Mother has taken to her bed and refuses to see visitors. Our family's reputation is in ruins."

"And all for what?" Lady Agnes asked, gesturing at the portfolio of documents they had rescued from the bank. "Evidence that may not even be sufficient to bring down our enemies."

The portfolio lay open on the table between them, its contents now seeming almost pathetic in light of what they had cost to obtain. Her father's coded journals, the inheritance documents, the witness statements—all of it felt inadequate against the magnitude of their losses.

"I keep wondering," Poppy said quietly, "whether we should have simply paid the blackmailer's demands and let the past remain buried."

"Perhaps," Lady Agnes agreed. "But then again, perhaps Lucy would still have died. Men like Redmayne don't simply disappear when inconvenient truths are suppressed. They find other ways to eliminate threats."

It was a cold comfort, but Poppy clung to it nonetheless. The alternative—that Lucy had died for nothing, that their pursuit of justice had been merely stubborn pride dressed up as principle—was too terrible to contemplate.

A soft knock at the library door interrupted their melancholy reflections. Mrs. Fletcher entered, her face bearing the sort of expression that promised more bad news.

"Begging your pardon," she said quietly, "but

there's a gentleman here to see you. Says he's from London, on official business."

Poppy and Lady Agnes exchanged glances. Official business could mean any number of things, none of them likely to be pleasant given their current circumstances.

"Show him in," Lady Agnes said with resignation.

The man who entered was perhaps forty years of age, dressed in the sort of respectable but unremarkable clothing favoured by government clerks. He carried a leather satchel and bore himself with the careful neutrality of someone accustomed to delivering unwelcome news.

"Lady Agnes Taverner? Miss Hartwell?" He bowed slightly as they acknowledged him. "I am Mr. Cornelius Ashby, representing the office of the Lord Chancellor. I'm afraid I bring word of some... developments concerning your recent activities."

"What sort of developments?" Poppy asked, though she dreaded the answer.

Mr. Ashby opened his satchel and withdrew a sheaf of official-looking documents. "It has come to the attention of certain parties that you have been making allegations against Lord Redmayne regarding matters of inheritance fraud. These allegations have been deemed sufficiently serious to warrant official inquiry."

For a moment, Poppy felt a surge of hope. If the government was finally taking their evidence seriously...

"However," Mr. Ashby continued, dashing her optimism, "Lord Redmayne has filed counter-accusations of criminal libel against both the Taverner and Hartwell families. He claims that you have been engaged in a conspiracy to defame his character using forged documents and false witness testimony."

The blood drained from Poppy's face. "That's preposterous. We have evidence—"

"Evidence that Lord Redmayne claims was fabricated by Miss Hartwell's late father as part of a scheme to extort money from respectable families." Mr. Ashby's tone was apologetic but firm. "I'm afraid the courts have issued warrants for your arrest on charges of conspiracy, libel, and attempted extortion."

Lady Agnes rose from her chair with regal dignity, though Poppy could see the strain around her eyes. "I see. And when are we expected to surrender ourselves to face these charges?"

"The warrants are to be executed immediately,"

Mr. Ashby replied. "I have constables waiting outside to escort you to London."

The trap was complete, then. Redmayne had used their own evidence against them, turning their accusations into proof of criminal conspiracy. With Lucy dead and their documents suspect, they had no way to prove their innocence.

"May we at least inform Mr. Taverner of these developments?" Poppy asked.

"Mr. Taverner is included in the warrants," Mr. Ashby said gently. "Though I understand he is... indisposed following recent tragic events."

As if summoned by the conversation, Edward appeared in the doorway. He looked haggard and hollow-eyed, but the mention of warrants had apparently penetrated his grief-induced stupor.

"What warrants?" he asked, his voice hoarse from disuse.

Mr. Ashby repeated his explanation while Edward listened with growing comprehension. When the clerk finished, Edward laughed—a sound devoid of humour or hope.

"Of course," he said bitterly. "Of course Redmayne would find a way to turn our evidence against us. I should have anticipated this."

"Edward," Poppy began, but he cut her off with a gesture.

"No, it's brilliant really. Use our own investigation to prove that we're criminals. Paint us as conspirators who fabricated evidence to extort money from innocent victims. Who would believe the word of a disgraced barrister and a desperate spinster against a peer of the realm?"

"The evidence will speak for itself," Lady Agnes said firmly. "In a proper court, with competent representation—"

"There will be no proper court," Edward interrupted. "Redmayne owns half the judges in London and has leverage over the other half. We'll be tried, convicted, and imprisoned before we can even present our defence."

Mr. Ashby cleared his throat uncomfortably. "If I might suggest, the Lord Chancellor's office is prepared to consider leniency in exchange for full cooperation. If you were to publicly retract your allegations and turn over all documents related to this matter..."

"You mean surrender," Edward said flatly.

"I mean accept that sometimes discretion is the better part of valour."

For a long moment, the library was silent except

for the ticking of the mantel clock and the distant sound of wind through the charred ruins of the east wing. Poppy found herself thinking of Lucy's bright smile, of her father's careful documentation of corruption, of all the innocents who had suffered while men like Redmayne prospered.

"No," she said quietly, surprising herself with the firmness in her voice.

"I beg your pardon?" Mr. Ashby asked.

"No," Poppy repeated, rising from her chair. "We will not surrender. We will not retract our allegations. And we will not allow the truth to be buried simply because powerful men find it inconvenient."

Edward stared at her with something approaching amazement. "Poppy, you don't understand what you're saying. They'll destroy you completely."

"They've already destroyed everything that matters," she replied, thinking of Rose's broken engagement, her mother's illness, Lucy's death. "What more can they take from us?"

Lady Agnes moved to stand beside her, her expression resolute despite the obvious cost of their defiance. "The girl is right. We have already paid too high a price to surrender now."

"Very well," Mr. Ashby said with obvious reluctance. "Then I'm afraid you leave me no choice."

He gestured toward the door, where the sound of heavy footsteps announced the arrival of the constables. As they entered the library, Poppy felt a strange sense of calm settle over her.

They might be defeated, but they would not be dishonoured. Whatever came next, whatever punishment Redmayne's influence could inflict upon them, they would face it with their integrity intact.

But even as she prepared to surrender herself to arrest, a new thought began to form in the back of her mind. Among her mother's old papers, locked away in Belmont House, lay documents that might change everything—if only she could find a way to reach them.

Her mother's birth records, which she had discovered weeks ago but barely examined in the rush of subsequent events. Documents that suggested Lady Catherine Hartwell had been born not to a respectable middle-class family, as they had always believed, but to someone of far more significant standing.

Someone whose name, if Poppy remembered correctly, had been Catherine Ashford.

The same family name that Mr. Aldridge had

mentioned as the rightful heir to Redmayne's stolen inheritance.

As the constables moved to place her in custody, Poppy smiled for the first time since Lucy's death. Perhaps their battle was not over after all.

CHAPTER 15

⁓

The journey to London in the custody of the constables passed in a haze of unreality. Poppy found herself chained to Lady Agnes in the back of a prison wagon, while Edward sat opposite them in similar restraints, his face a mask of bitter resignation. The man who had once fought so passionately for justice now seemed utterly defeated, worn down by grief and the weight of accumulated failures.

"Edward," Poppy said softly as the wagon jolted over the rutted roads, "there may yet be hope. The documents I mentioned—my mother's birth records—"

"Hope?" Edward's laugh was harsh and broken. "Poppy, we are being taken to face charges of criminal conspiracy against one of the most powerful men in England. Whatever documents you think you possess will be dismissed as further evidence of our criminal intent."

Lady Agnes shifted uncomfortably in her shackles. "Perhaps if we could get word to Inspector Bradbury—"

"Bradbury cannot help us now," Edward interrupted. "If he could have acted against Redmayne, he would have done so years ago. The fact that we are here, in chains, proves that corruption reaches deeper than any of us imagined."

The despair in his voice was palpable, and Poppy felt her own determination wavering. Perhaps he was right. Perhaps their pursuit of justice had been nothing more than futile idealism, doomed from the start.

But then she thought of Lucy's bright courage, of her father's careful documentation of truth, of all the innocents who would continue to suffer if men like Redmayne remained unchallenged. Whatever her own fate might be, she could not simply surrender.

The Tower of London loomed before them as evening fell, its ancient stones seeming to absorb what little light remained in the grey sky. The sight of the fortress-prison sent a chill through Poppy that had nothing to do with the autumn air.

"Hardly the sort of accommodation one expects for political prisoners," Lady Agnes observed with bitter irony as they were roughly escorted through the gates.

"Political prisoners have rights," one of their guards replied with obvious satisfaction. "Criminal conspirators have considerably fewer."

They were separated immediately upon arrival—Edward to the men's quarters, while Poppy and Lady Agnes were taken to a cramped cell in what had once housed traitors and enemies of the state. The symbolism was not lost on any of them.

The cell itself was a study in medieval brutality barely softened by centuries of supposed civilisation. Stone walls wept with perpetual dampness, a single barred window provided minimal light, and the straw on the floor had clearly not been changed in recent memory. A bucket in the corner served purposes that Poppy preferred not to contemplate.

"Well," Lady Agnes said with forced lightness as the heavy door clanged shut behind them, "at least we have each other for company."

But Poppy barely heard her. The reality of their situation was beginning to sink in with crushing finality. They were imprisoned, cut off from any possibility of mounting a defence, while Redmayne's network moved freely to consolidate their victory.

"My family," she whispered, sinking onto the narrow bench that served as the cell's only furniture. "What will happen to Rose and Mother when news of our arrest becomes public?"

"Nothing good," Lady Agnes replied with characteristic honesty. "Though perhaps they will be safer with us out of the way. Redmayne's quarrel was primarily with our investigation, not with innocent family members."

The first night in the Tower passed in a sleepless haze of anxiety and discomfort. When dawn finally crept through their barred window, it brought with it a visitor neither of them had expected.

Mr. Bradshaw, Redmayne's chief lieutenant, appeared at their cell door accompanied by a pair of guards. His expression carried the satisfaction of a man who had achieved a long-sought victory.

"Miss Hartwell, Lady Agnes," he said with mock courtesy. "I trust your accommodations are... adequate?"

"What do you want?" Poppy asked, too exhausted for politeness.

"To offer you one final opportunity for redemption," Bradshaw replied. "Lord Redmayne is prepared to be magnanimous in victory. If you will sign confessions admitting to your crimes and publicly apologising for your false accusations, he is willing to ensure that your sentences are... reduced."

"Reduced to what?" Lady Agnes asked sharply.

"Transportation rather than hanging," Bradshaw said with casual cruelty. "A life of hard labour in the colonies rather than the gallows. Surely a generous offer under the circumstances."

The offer hung in the stifling air of the cell like a physical presence. Transportation to the penal colonies meant effective exile from everything they had ever known, but it also meant survival. Death would serve no one's interests except their enemies.

"And if we refuse?" Poppy asked.

"Then you will face the full weight of English justice. The evidence against you is overwhelming— forged documents, false testimony, conspiracy to extort money from a peer of the realm. The penalty for such crimes is death."

"Evidence that you manufactured," Lady Agnes said coldly.

"Evidence that exists, regardless of its origins," Bradshaw corrected. "The courts care about proof, not provenance."

He produced a document from his coat and slid it through the bars. "You have until tomorrow evening to consider the offer. I suggest you use the time wisely."

After he departed, Poppy and Lady Agnes sat in silence, staring at the confession that would save their lives at the cost of their honour. The document was comprehensive in its self-condemnation, admitting not only to the charges against them but also to a fictional conspiracy spanning years.

"He wants us to confess to crimes we never committed," Poppy said finally.

"He wants us to publicly validate his version of events," Lady Agnes corrected. "Our confessions would not only clear Redmayne of any wrongdoing but also serve as a warning to others who might consider challenging powerful interests."

"Would anyone believe such confessions?"

"People believe what they wish to believe, particularly when the alternative requires them to question the legitimacy of the systems they depend upon."

As the day wore on, their situation seemed increasingly hopeless. No visitors came to offer legal representation or support. No word arrived from Edward about his own circumstances. They were effectively cut off from the outside world, left to contemplate their bleak choice between dishonour and death.

But as evening approached, Poppy found herself thinking not of their immediate predicament but of the larger pattern of events that had brought them to this point. Her father's death, Sebastian's "accident," Lucy's tragic end in the fire—all of them convenient for Redmayne's interests, all of them removing threats to his network of corruption.

"Lady Agnes," she said suddenly, "there's something that's been troubling me about the sequence of events."

"What do you mean?"

"The timing of everything. My father's death came just as he was preparing to expose the inheritance fraud. Sebastian died when he began investigating railway investments. And Lucy..."

"Lucy died when we were closest to assembling complete evidence against Redmayne," Lady Agnes finished grimly. "Yes, the pattern is rather obvious once one looks for it."

"But that means there's someone within our circle—someone who has been reporting our activities to Redmayne's people from the very beginning."

"Someone who knew about Sebastian's investigation, who knew about your father's journals, who knew exactly when we would be returning to Taverner Hall."

The implications were staggering. Someone they had trusted had been systematically betraying them, providing their enemies with the information needed to stay one step ahead of their investigation.

"But who?" Poppy asked. "Mr. Aldridge seemed genuinely terrified. Jenkins has been loyal to my family for decades. Inspector Bradbury—"

"Has been remarkably ineffective despite years of supposedly investigating Redmayne's activities," Lady Agnes pointed out. "Perhaps his loyalty is not what we assumed."

The possibility that they had been betrayed by the very man who claimed to be fighting their cause sent a fresh wave of despair through Poppy. If even Scotland Yard was compromised, then their situation was truly hopeless.

But even as she contemplated the depths of their betrayal, another thought began to form. If their investigation had been monitored so closely, if their enemies knew their every move, then perhaps there was information that could be turned to their advantage.

"Lady Agnes," she said slowly, "when you were

supposedly cooperating with Redmayne's network, what exactly did you tell them about our activities?"

"Only what was necessary to maintain my position within their confidence. Why?"

"Because if they believed you were truly working for them, they might have revealed information about their own operations. Details that could be useful if we ever found a way to turn the tables."

Lady Agnes was quiet for a long moment, her dark eyes reflecting the dim light from their barred window. "There was one thing," she said finally. "A name that came up repeatedly in their conversations. Someone they referred to as their 'insurance policy' within the government."

"What sort of insurance policy?"

"Someone highly placed, someone with access to sensitive information about investigations and legal proceedings. Someone who could ensure that inconvenient evidence disappeared and that awkward witnesses were silenced."

"Do you know who it is?"

"I was never told directly, but from the context..." Lady Agnes paused, seeming to weigh her words carefully. "I believe it may be someone within the Lord Chancellor's office itself."

The revelation struck Poppy like a physical blow.

If Redmayne had an ally within the highest levels of the legal system, then their arrest and imprisonment had been orchestrated from the very beginning. Their enemies had not simply reacted to their investigation—they had controlled it from the start.

"Then we never had a chance," she whispered.

"Perhaps not," Lady Agnes agreed. "But knowledge of such corruption might be valuable to the right people. The question is whether we can find a way to get that information to someone who would act upon it."

As night fell over the Tower of London, Poppy found herself clinging to this one slender thread of possibility. They might be defeated, they might be facing death or exile, but perhaps their story could still serve some purpose.

The confession document lay on the bench between them, waiting for their signatures. Tomorrow evening, they would have to choose between honour and survival, between truth and expediency.

But for now, in the darkness of their cell, Poppy allowed herself to imagine that their fight for justice might yet have meaning, even if they would not live to see its ultimate victory.

CHAPTER 16

$\mathcal{T}$he second day of their imprisonment brought an unexpected visitor to the Tower. Poppy was summoned from her cell in the early afternoon, her wrists shackled as she was escorted through the ancient corridors to a small chamber that had been set aside for meetings between prisoners and their legal representatives.

She expected to find a barrister sent by some charitable organization, or perhaps a clerk bearing more threats from Redmayne's network. Instead, she found Edward waiting for her, looking haggard but more alert than he had been since Lucy's death.

"Edward!" she exclaimed, relief flooding through her at the sight of him alive and apparently unharmed. "I was so worried—"

"As was I," he replied, rising as she entered. The guard who had escorted her remained by the door, but at least they were permitted to speak freely. "Poppy, there have been developments. Significant ones."

"What sort of developments?"

Edward's pale eyes held a glimmer of something she hadn't seen there since before the fire—hope, perhaps, or at least grim determination. "I've had a visitor. Someone you would not expect."

"Who?"

"Mr. Jonathan Hartley, the journalist Lucy mentioned. It seems our situation has attracted more attention than we realized."

Poppy felt her heart quicken. "What did he want?"

"To verify certain information about Redmayne's network. Apparently, he has been investigating the same corruption we uncovered, but from a different angle. Our arrest has confirmed suspicions he's harboured for some time."

"Can he help us?"

Edward's expression grew troubled. "Perhaps. But not in the way we might hope. Hartley cannot simply publish accusations without concrete proof, and our evidence has been dismissed as fabricated. However..."

He paused, glancing at the guard before continuing in a lower voice.

"Hartley has offered to publish our story if we can provide him with information that goes beyond what Redmayne's people already know. Details about the network's operations, names of conspirators, evidence of corruption within the government itself."

"Information that could cost us our lives if Redmayne discovered we had shared it."

"Yes. But information that might also serve a greater purpose than our individual survival."

Poppy studied Edward's face, noting the way he held himself. There was a resolve there that she hadn't seen since before their world began crumbling around them.

"There's something else, isn't there?" she asked.

"Lord Redmayne himself wishes to see you."

The words struck her like a physical blow. "What?"

"A formal request came through official channels this morning. Lord Redmayne has asked for a private audience with you specifically. The authorities have granted permission, given that you are technically charged with crimes against his person."

"Why would he want to see me?"

"I suspect," Edward said grimly, "because he wishes to make you an offer. Something he cannot risk putting in writing or communicating through intermediaries."

The implications sent a chill through Poppy's veins. If Redmayne wanted to see her personally, it could only mean that their investigation had threatened him in ways that went beyond what they had imagined.

"When?" she asked.

"This evening. But Poppy, you must understand —this could be a trap. Redmayne may intend to eliminate you quietly, claiming you attacked him or attempted to escape."

"Or he may have something to offer that he believes I cannot refuse."

Edward reached across the small table and grasped her hands, his touch warm despite the cold iron of their shackles. "Whatever he offers you, whatever threats he makes, remember that some prices are too high to pay."

"Even if the price is our lives?"

"Especially then."

That evening, as twilight settled over London, Poppy was escorted from the Tower to an unmarked carriage. Her destination proved to be a private club in St. James's, the sort of establishment where powerful men gathered to conduct business away from prying eyes.

She was led through opulent corridors lined with portraits of long-dead statesmen and military heroes, finally arriving at a small private dining room where Lord Redmayne waited alone.

The man himself was not as imposing as she had expected. Of medium height and unremarkable appearance, he might have been any prosperous gentleman of middle years. Only his eyes betrayed the ruthless intelligence that had built his empire of corruption.

"Miss Hartwell," he said, rising courteously as she entered. "Thank you for accepting my invitation. Please, be seated."

She remained standing, acutely aware of the guards who had taken positions by the door. "I hardly had a choice in the matter."

"Everyone has choices, my dear. The question is whether they have the wisdom to make the right ones." He gestured to the chair opposite his own. "Please. I have taken the liberty of ordering dinner. Even prisoners must eat."

Reluctantly, Poppy seated herself, noting that her shackles had been removed for the duration of the meeting. The gesture was clearly meant to suggest that she was a guest rather than a captive, though the armed guards made the reality clear enough.

"You have caused me considerable inconvenience," Redmayne said conversationally as servants appeared to serve the meal. "Your father's journals, the bank documents, your investigation into matters that should have remained buried. Most troublesome."

"The truth has a way of surfacing eventually," Poppy replied, testing the limits of his patience.

"Does it? I have found that truth is remarkably malleable, particularly when shaped by those with sufficient resources and influence." He cut into his beef with precise movements. "But you have proven more... persistent than anticipated."

"My persistence, as you call it, has landed me in the Tower facing charges of conspiracy. Hardly a threat to your position."

"On the contrary, my dear Miss Hartwell. Your arrest has created exactly the sort of public attention I prefer to avoid. Questions are being asked in Parliament. Journalists are investigating. Your martyrdom, if I may call it that, serves my enemies far better than your freedom ever did."

The admission surprised her with its frankness.

"Then why not simply have me quietly murdered? Surely that would be simpler than this elaborate charade."

Redmayne smiled, and the expression was genuinely chilling. "Because I believe we can reach an understanding that serves both our interests. You see, I have recently learned something about your family that I think you will find most illuminating."

He reached into his coat and withdrew a folder, placing it on the table between them. "Your mother's birth records, properly investigated. Most fascinating reading."

Poppy's heart raced, but she forced herself to remain calm. "I'm not sure what you mean."

"Come now, Miss Hartwell. We both know that you have discovered your mother's connection to the Ashford family. What you may not realize is the full extent of what that connection means."

He opened the folder, revealing documents that appeared to be official birth and marriage records. "Lady Catherine Ashford, as she was born, was not merely connected to the family that rightfully owns my current estates. She was the direct heir, the legitimate daughter of the Eighth Earl of Ashford."

The revelation struck Poppy like a physical blow.

If her mother was the rightful heir to Redmayne's stolen inheritance, then...

"Which makes you, my dear," Redmayne continued with obvious satisfaction, "the current rightful heir to the Ashford title and estates. Including, I might add, properties worth approximately half a million pounds."

The room seemed to spin around Poppy as the implications sank in. She was not merely investigating inheritance fraud—she was the victim of it.

"Of course," Redmayne continued smoothly, "establishing such a claim would require extensive legal proceedings. Years of litigation, massive expenses, and the sort of public scrutiny that tends to destroy families caught in its path. Your sister's reputation, your mother's health—both would likely be casualties of such a prolonged battle."

"What are you proposing?" Poppy asked, though she dreaded the answer.

"A private settlement. I retain the titles and properties I have worked so hard to maintain, while you and your family receive a generous compensation for any... inconvenience. Enough to restore your family's reputation, secure your sister's future, and ensure your mother's comfort for the remainder of her life."

"In exchange for?"

"Your silence, naturally. A formal statement that your accusations against me were the result of misunderstandings and grief-induced confusion. A public apology that puts an end to this unfortunate affair."

The offer hung in the air between them like a poisonous cloud. Everything she had fought for, everything that had cost Lucy her life and Edward his remaining hope, reduced to a business transaction.

"How much?" she asked quietly.

"Fifty thousand pounds. More than enough to rebuild your family's fortunes and secure their future prosperity."

"And if I refuse?"

Redmayne's expression hardened. "Then you will face trial, conviction, and execution for crimes against the Crown. Your family will be ruined by association, your mother will die of shame and despair, and your sister will spend her life as a pariah. And in the end, the truth you claim to champion will die with you."

"While you continue to profit from stolen inheritance."

"While I continue to manage estates and

resources that have flourished under my steward-ship. Tell me, Miss Hartwell, what good would it do anyone for you to claim properties you have no experience managing, titles you have no training to bear? Your mother has lived her entire life as a gentleman's daughter. Would you really inflict the burden of nobility upon her in her declining years?"

The argument was seductive in its logic, and Poppy found herself wavering despite her convictions. Was her pursuit of abstract justice worth destroying everyone she loved?

"I need time to consider," she said finally.

"Time is a luxury I cannot afford to grant," Redmayne replied. "Your trial begins tomorrow. If you accept my offer, I can arrange for the charges to be quietly dropped on the grounds of insufficient evidence. If you refuse..."

He spread his hands in a gesture of regret that was entirely false.

"Your decision, Miss Hartwell. But I would suggest you think carefully about what truly matters to you—idealistic principles, or the welfare of those you claim to love."

As the guards prepared to escort her back to the Tower, Poppy felt the weight of impossible choice settling over her like a shroud. Edward had warned her that some prices were too high to pay, but what if the price of refusal was the destruction of everyone she held dear?

The carriage ride back to prison passed in a blur of agonized indecision. By the time she reached her cell, where Lady Agnes waited anxiously for news, Poppy was no closer to an answer than when she had left.

But one thing had become clear during her meeting with Redmayne: their enemy was far more dangerous than they had realized, and far more desperate. The very fact that he was willing to offer such generous terms suggested that their investigation had struck closer to his heart than she had dared hope.

The question now was whether that knowledge would prove to be salvation or merely a more elaborate form of destruction.

CHAPTER 17

*P*oppy returned to her cell in the Tower with her mind reeling from Redmayne's revelation and his impossible offer. The knowledge that she was the rightful heir to the very estates he had stolen should have felt like vindication, but instead it only deepened her sense of despair. What good was a claim to nobility when she was likely to face the gallows before she could assert it?

Lady Agnes took one look at her face and immediately moved to the small bench they shared.

"What did he tell you?" she asked quietly.

As Poppy recounted the meeting, she watched Lady Agnes's expression grow increasingly troubled.

When she finished, the older woman sat in silence for several minutes, her dark eyes fixed on the barred window that showed only a small patch of darkening sky.

"Fifty thousand pounds," Lady Agnes said finally. "A fortune by any measure."

"Blood money," Poppy replied bitterly. "Payment for my silence while he continues to profit from theft."

"Perhaps. But also the salvation of your family. Your mother's health, your sister's future—these are not abstract concepts, Poppy. They are real people who will suffer real consequences if you choose martyrdom over pragmatism."

The words stung because they echoed Poppy's own tormented thoughts. "You think I should accept his offer?"

"I think," Lady Agnes said carefully, "that you should consider whether your father would have wanted you to sacrifice everything he loved for the sake of principles he can no longer benefit from."

Before Poppy could respond, the sound of footsteps echoed in the corridor outside their cell. The heavy door swung open to reveal a guard, but instead of the routine inspection she expected, he stepped aside to admit a figure that made her heart leap with hope and fear in equal measure.

Edward entered the cell, but something in his bearing immediately set her on edge. He moved with the careful precision of a man under enormous strain, and his pale eyes seemed to avoid meeting hers directly.

"Edward," she said, rising from the bench. "What brings you here? Has something happened?"

"Several things," he replied, his voice unnaturally formal. "I've been permitted to speak with you about... arrangements for tomorrow's proceedings."

"Arrangements?"

Edward finally met her gaze, and what she saw there made her blood run cold. "Poppy, there are things I need to tell you. Things about Lady Agnes, about my family, about choices that were made long before we ever met."

Lady Agnes had gone very still, her face pale in the dim light. "Edward, perhaps this is not the time—"

"No," he said sharply. "It is precisely the time. Poppy deserves to know the truth before she makes any decisions about her future."

He moved closer, his movements restless and agitated. "Lady Agnes, would you care to explain to

Miss Hartwell exactly how Sebastian died? The real circumstances, not the fiction you've been maintaining?"

"Edward, please," Lady Agnes whispered.

"Sebastian wasn't investigating railway investments when he died," Edward continued relentlessly. "He was trying to cover up his own involvement in Redmayne's network. My brother, Poppy, was one of the conspirators."

The revelation struck Poppy like a physical blow. "That's impossible. You said he was fighting against corruption—"

"I said what I believed to be true. What Lady Agnes allowed me to believe." Edward's voice was raw with pain and anger. "But Sebastian wasn't a victim of Redmayne's network—he was a willing participant. Isn't that right, Agnes?"

Lady Agnes seemed to crumble before their eyes, her regal composure finally breaking completely. "You don't understand," she said, her voice barely above a whisper. "Sebastian was trying to protect the family. We were facing bankruptcy, complete ruin. The investments he made with Redmayne were meant to save us."

"By helping to defraud innocent people?"

"By participating in financial arrangements that

were... morally questionable but legally defensible." Lady Agnes looked up at Poppy with desperate eyes. "Sebastian convinced himself that no one was truly being harmed, that the money would be better managed by Redmayne than by the rightful heirs."

"Until he discovered that one of those rightful heirs was my mother," Poppy said, the pieces falling into place with horrible clarity.

"Yes. When Sebastian learned that Lady Catherine Ashford—your mother—was still alive and had children, he realized the full implications of what he had done. He tried to withdraw from the arrangement, but by then he knew too much."

"So they killed him."

"So they arranged for him to have an accident while he was drunk and distraught," Lady Agnes corrected. "I was there, Poppy. I watched it happen, and I did nothing to stop it."

The confession hung in the stifling air of the cell like a poison cloud. Edward's face had gone ashen, and Poppy could see the final destruction of his illusions about his brother playing out in his pale eyes.

"Why?" he asked, his voice breaking. "Why didn't you tell me the truth?"

"Because I couldn't bear to destroy your memory of him completely," Lady Agnes replied. "Sebastian was weak, and greedy, and foolish—but he wasn't evil. In the end, he tried to do the right thing, and it cost him his life."

"And you've been protecting his reputation ever since."

"I've been protecting this family's honour," Lady Agnes said with a flash of her old spirit. "What good would it have done to expose Sebastian's crimes after his death? It would only have provided Redmayne with more leverage over us."

Edward turned away, his shoulders shaking with suppressed emotion. When he finally spoke again, his voice was barely audible.

"There's more, isn't there? About your cooperation with Redmayne's people, about the information you've been feeding them."

Lady Agnes nodded miserably. "When they approached me after Sebastian's death, they offered a bargain. Silence about his involvement in exchange for... intelligence about any attempts to investigate their operations."

"You've been spying on us from the beginning."

"I've been trying to protect what remained of our family. But when Lucy died..." Lady Agnes broke down completely, great sobs wracking her small frame. "When that beautiful, innocent child

died because of my betrayals, I knew I couldn't
continue."

Poppy sank back onto the bench, overwhelmed
by the magnitude of the deceptions that had
surrounded their investigation. "The midnight
meeting I overheard at Taverner Hall—you weren't
coordinating with Inspector Bradbury, were you?"

"No. I was reporting to one of Redmayne's agents
about your progress in decoding the journals."

"And the fire?"

"Was meant to destroy evidence, yes." Lady Agnes
looked up with haunted eyes. "I didn't know that
Lucy would run into the house. I swear to you, I
never intended for her to be harmed."

The cell fell silent except for Lady Agnes's quiet
weeping and the distant sounds of the Tower's
evening routine. Poppy felt as though everything she
had believed about their mission, their allies, their
very purpose had been built on lies.

"Why are you telling me this now?" she asked
Edward.

He turned back to face her, and she was shocked
by the anguish in his expression. "Because
Redmayne has made me an offer as well. My freedom, and the promise that the Taverner name will
be cleared of any association with scandal, in

exchange for testifying against you at tomorrow's trial."

"Edward, no."

"He wants me to confirm that your father's journals were forgeries, that you manipulated me into supporting your false accusations against him. In exchange, I would be portrayed as another victim of your elaborate conspiracy."

"But you won't do it," Poppy said, though something in his tone made her suddenly uncertain.

"Won't I?" Edward's laugh was bitter and broken. "My brother was a criminal who betrayed everything our family stood for. My aunt has been spying on us for our enemies. The woman I love is about to be executed for crimes she committed in pursuit of justice that may not even exist. Tell me, Poppy— what exactly do I have left to lose?"

"Your honour," she said quietly. "Your integrity. The very things that made me fall in love with you."

The words hung between them, the first public acknowledgment of feelings that had been building for months. Edward stared at her as though she had struck him.

"My honour?" he repeated. "My integrity? Poppy, I have been a fool from the very beginning. Every principle I thought I was fighting for, every cause I believed in—all of it has been corrupted by lies and self-deception."

"That doesn't mean you have to abandon them now."

"Doesn't it? What good are principles if maintaining them means watching the people you love suffer and die for nothing?"

Lady Agnes looked up from her grief, her eyes moving between them. "There is another way," she said quietly.

"What do you mean?" Poppy asked.

"I mean that perhaps it's time for the truth—all of it—to finally come to light." Lady Agnes struggled to her feet, her demeanour suddenly determined. "Sebastian's involvement in the conspiracy, my betrayals, Redmayne's crimes—everything."

"Agnes, that would destroy what's left of our family's reputation," Edward protested.

"Our family's reputation is already destroyed," she replied with calm finality. "But perhaps its sacrifice could serve some greater purpose. If I were to confess publicly to my role in this conspiracy, if I were to provide testimony about Redmayne's network and methods..."

"They would execute you," Poppy said.

"Probably. But they might spare you and Edward.

And more importantly, the truth would finally be told."

Edward stared at his aunt as though seeing her clearly for the first time. "You would do that? After everything you've done to protect the family name?"

"The family name is already lost," Lady Agnes said with quiet dignity. "But perhaps some measure of honour can still be salvaged from the wreckage."

She moved to the barred window, looking out at the night sky above London. "Tomorrow, when they bring me to testify against you, I will instead tell the court everything I know about Lord Redmayne's network. Every crime, every conspiracy, every name I can remember."

"They'll never believe you," Edward said. "They'll claim you're lying to save us."

"Then that will be for others to judge," Lady Agnes replied. "But at least the truth will be spoken, even if justice remains elusive."

As she spoke, Poppy felt something shift inside her—a sense of hope that she had thought lost forever. Not hope for their personal salvation, but hope that their struggle might yet serve some purpose beyond their own survival.

The game had been rigged against them from the beginning, their enemies had controlled the board at every move, but perhaps there was still one final gambit they could play.

If Lady Agnes was willing to sacrifice herself for the truth, then perhaps their fight had not been in vain after all.

CHAPTER 18

The morning of their trial dawned grey and cold, with a bitter wind that seemed to penetrate even the ancient stones of the Tower. Poppy had slept little, her mind churning with the revelations of the previous evening and the impossible choices that lay ahead. Lady Agnes's offer of self-sacrifice had provided a glimmer of hope, but it came at a price that seemed almost too high to accept.

As she prepared for what might be her final day of freedom, Poppy found herself thinking not of the grand principles that had driven their investigation, but of simple, human connections—her mother's gentle wisdom, Rose's bright laughter, even Lucy's fierce courage that had cost her so dearly.

"You're thinking of your family," Lady Agnes observed as they were led from their cell toward the prison wagon that would transport them to the Old Bailey.

"Among other things," Poppy replied. "I keep wondering what my father would have made of all this. Whether he would be proud of our pursuit of justice or appalled by its consequences."

"Perhaps both," Lady Agnes said with a sad smile. "The best of us contain contradictions, after all."

The journey through London's streets was a surreal experience. Despite the early hour, crowds had gathered along their route—some curious, some hostile, others seeming to regard them with a sympathy that suggested not everyone believed the official version of their crimes.

"Look there," Lady Agnes said quietly, nodding toward a group of well-dressed women who had positioned themselves near the courthouse steps. "I believe we may have attracted more support than we realized."

As their wagon drew closer, Poppy could see that the women carried signs bearing messages of support for justice and reform. Among them, she was surprised to recognize several faces from London society—ladies who had attended the same salons and tea parties where she had once played the role of Edward's devoted fiancée.

"Lady Pemberton," she whispered, spotting the hostess who had first welcomed her and Edward as an engaged couple. "And Mrs. Aldrich. I never expected..."

"Perhaps our investigation has inspired others to question the comfortable assumptions of their world," Lady Agnes suggested. "Sometimes truth has a way of spreading beyond the intentions of those who first speak it."

They were separated again upon reaching the courthouse, with Lady Agnes being led to a holding area for witnesses while Poppy was taken to the dock where she would stand trial alongside Edward. The courtroom itself was packed with spectators, the galleries filled with a mixture of London society and common citizens drawn by the sensational nature of the charges.

Edward was already seated in the dock when she arrived, his face pale but composed. He looked up as she took her place beside him, and for a moment their eyes met with an intensity that spoke of every-thing they had shared and everything they stood to lose.

"Whatever happens today," he said quietly, "I want

you to know that I regret nothing about our partnership. You have shown me what it means to fight for something greater than oneself."

Before Poppy could respond, the court was called to order and Lord Justice Blackwood took his seat at the bench. The judge was a formidable figure in his scarlet robes and white wig, his stern expression suggesting little sympathy for the accused.

"The Crown versus Hartwell and Taverner," the clerk announced. "Charges of conspiracy, criminal libel, and attempted extortion against Lord Redmayne."

Mr. prosecuting counsel, a thin man with sharp features and a voice like a blade, rose to present the case against them. His opening statement was a masterpiece of character assassination, painting Poppy as a desperate spinster driven to crime by financial need and Edward as a disgraced barrister seeking revenge against the legal establishment that had rejected him.

"These defendants," the prosecutor declared, "represent the worst sort of criminals—those who would use false accusations and forged documents to destroy the reputation of an innocent peer of the realm. Their conspiracy was elaborate, their methods ruthless, and their motives entirely self-serving."

As he spoke, Poppy glanced around the courtroom, noting the faces of those in attendance. Redmayne himself sat in the front row, his expression one of injured dignity, while his associates occupied strategic positions throughout the gallery. But she also spotted some unexpected allies—journalists with notebooks at the ready, reformist politicians who had been investigating corruption in their own right, and even some members of the clergy who had spoken out against social injustice.

The prosecution's case proceeded with mechanical efficiency. Document after document was presented as evidence of their supposed crimes, while witness after witness testified to their suspicious behaviour and alleged misconduct. The picture that emerged was one of calculated deception spanning months of careful planning.

But when Mr. Aldridge was called to testify, Poppy noticed something unexpected. The elderly clerk appeared nervous beyond what the circumstances warranted, his hands shaking as he was sworn in and his voice barely audible as he began to speak.

"You were present at Rothschild's Bank when the defendants attempted to access certain documents," the prosecutor prompted.

"Yes, sir," Mr. Aldridge replied, but his eyes kept darting toward the public gallery where several men Poppy didn't recognize sat watching intently.

"And did Miss Hartwell claim that these documents belonged to her late father?"

"She did, sir, but—"

"A simple yes or no will suffice," the prosecutor interrupted sharply.

"Yes, sir."

"And in your professional opinion, were these documents authentic?"

Mr. Aldridge hesitated, his gaze moving from the prosecutor to the judge to the gallery and back again. "I... that is to say... the documents appeared to be..."

He trailed off, sweat beading on his forehead despite the cool temperature of the courtroom.

"Mr. Aldridge," Lord Justice Blackwood interjected, "you must speak clearly for the record."

"My lord," Mr. Aldridge said suddenly, his voice gaining strength, "I cannot in good conscience continue with this testimony."

A murmur ran through the courtroom, and the prosecutor's face darkened with anger. "What do you mean by that statement?"

"I mean, sir, that I have been instructed to provide false testimony regarding the authenticity of certain documents. I have been threatened with the loss of my position and worse if I do not corroborate the Crown's case against the defendants."

The courtroom erupted in shocked exclamations, and Lord Justice Blackwood's gavel rang out repeatedly as he called for order. "Mr. Aldridge, are you saying that you have been suborned to commit perjury?"

"Yes, my lord. The documents in question appeared to be entirely authentic, and Miss Hartwell's claim to them was legitimate based on the authorization she provided."

Poppy felt her heart leap with hope as she watched the prosecution's carefully constructed case begin to crumble. But her elation was short-lived as she noticed several of the unidentified men in the gallery rising from their seats and moving toward the exits.

Before anyone could react, one of these men had reached Mr. Aldridge's position. There was a brief scuffle, a sharp cry from the witness, and then Mr. Aldridge collapsed to the floor, clutching his chest.

"Murder!" someone shouted from the gallery. "They've poisoned him!"

Chaos erupted in the courtroom as spectators pushed toward the exits and court officials rushed to tend to the fallen witness. In the confusion, Poppy saw several more of Redmayne's associates attempting to slip away unnoticed.

But they had reckoned without the journalist Jonathan Hartley, who had positioned his own allies strategically throughout the room. As Redmayne's men tried to escape, they found their way blocked by determined reformers who had come prepared for exactly this sort of intimidation.

"Seize those men!" Hartley called out, pointing toward the fleeing suspects. "They are the ones responsible for this outrage!"

Lord Justice Blackwood's voice boomed over the disorder: "This court will not be intimidated by violence! Bailiffs, arrest anyone attempting to leave without permission!"

As order was gradually restored, it became clear that Mr. Aldridge, while injured, was still alive. The attack had been meant to silence him permanently, but quick intervention by court physicians had prevented the poison from proving fatal.

"My lord," Hartley said, rising from his seat in the gallery, "I request permission to address the court as a representative of the press. The events we have just witnessed demonstrate that this trial is part of a larger conspiracy to suppress the truth about corruption in the highest levels of society."

"This is highly irregular," the prosecutor protested.

"As is attempting to murder a witness in open court," Lord Justice Blackwood replied dryly. "Mr. Hartley, you may speak, but be brief."

Hartley moved to the centre of the courtroom, his presence commanding attention from every corner of the room. "My lord, for months I have been investigating allegations of systematic corruption involving forged inheritance documents, bribery of public officials, and the murder of those who sought to expose these crimes. The defendants in this case are not criminals—they are the victims of an elaborate conspiracy designed to silence them."

"You have evidence to support these claims?" the judge asked.

"I do, my lord. Evidence provided by Lady Agnes

Taverner, who wishes to make a full confession about her unwilling participation in this conspiracy."

As if summoned by his words, Lady Agnes appeared in the witness box, her bearing dignified despite her circumstances. She had clearly made peace with her decision to sacrifice herself for the truth.

"Lady Agnes," Hartley continued, "will you tell this court about your knowledge of Lord Redmayne's criminal network?"

"I will," Lady Agnes replied, her voice carrying clearly through the now-silent courtroom. "I will tell you everything."

As she began her testimony, detailing years of corruption, murder, and systematic fraud, Poppy felt a sense of vindication that went beyond their personal circumstances. The truth was finally being spoken in a forum where it could not be suppressed or discredited.

The battle was far from over, but for the first time since their investigation began, they were fighting on equal terms. Their enemies had been forced into the open, their methods exposed for all to see.

Whatever the ultimate outcome of the trial, their fight for justice had taken on a life of its own, inspiring others to question the comfortable assumptions of a corrupt system.

As Lady Agnes's clear voice filled the courtroom with devastating revelations about Redmayne's network, Poppy allowed herself to hope that perhaps their sacrifices had not been in vain after all.

CHAPTER 19

*L*ady Agnes's testimony had transformed the courtroom from a place of prosecution into a forum for revelation. As she spoke with calm precision about years of corruption, murder, and systematic fraud, Poppy watched the faces of those assembled and saw the tide of public opinion shifting before her eyes.

"Lord Redmayne approached me shortly after my Sebastian Tavener's death," Lady Agnes continued, her voice never wavering despite the magnitude of her confessions. "He offered protection from scandal in exchange for information about any attempts to investigate his network's activities."

The prosecutor had tried repeatedly to discredit her testimony, but each interruption only served to highlight the devastating nature of her revelations. Lord Justice Blackwood himself seemed transfixed by the scope of the conspiracy she was unveiling.

"You claim that Lord Redmayne was responsible for your Mr Tavener's death," the judge said. "Can you provide specific details about how this was accomplished?"

"Sebastian had discovered that the railway investments he had been persuaded to support were part of a larger scheme to defraud legitimate heirs of their inheritance. When he threatened to expose the conspiracy, he was encouraged to drink heavily and then... allowed to have what appeared to be a riding accident."

"Allowed?"

"I was present, my lord. I watched as Sebastian's horse was deliberately startled while he was in no condition to control it. When he fell, those responsible made no attempt to render aid. Instead, they ensured that he could not survive to tell his story."

A gasp ran through the courtroom, and Poppy saw Lord Redmayne's face drain of colour. For the first time since the trial began, his mask of injured dignity had slipped to reveal something approaching panic.

"This is preposterous!" he called out from his seat

in the gallery. "The ravings of a grief-stricken woman who seeks to deflect blame for her own criminal activities!"

But his protest only drew attention to his presence, and several spectators turned to study him with newfound suspicion. Jonathan Hartley was frantically taking notes, his pen moving across the page as he recorded every word for posterity.

"Lord Redmayne," Lady Agnes continued, turning to face him directly, "also ordered the fire at Taverner Hall that claimed the life of Miss Lucy Taverner. He was desperate to destroy any evidence in our possession."

The accusation hit the courtroom like a thunderbolt. The murder of an innocent young woman was beyond what even Redmayne's supporters could stomach, and Poppy could see his remaining allies beginning to distance themselves from him.

"You have no proof of such an outrageous allegation," the prosecutor sputtered, though his confidence was clearly shaken.

"Don't I?" Lady Agnes reached into her reticule and withdrew a small leather journal. "Sebastian kept detailed records of his involvement with the network, including correspondence with Lord

Redmayne. I have preserved these documents as... insurance."

She handed the journal to a court bailiff, who passed it to Lord Justice Blackwood. As the judge examined its contents, his expression grew increasingly grave.

"These appear to be authentic," he said finally. "Letters bearing Lord Redmayne's seal and signature, detailing plans for various fraudulent activities."

"Forgeries!" Redmayne shouted, rising from his seat. "Elaborate forgeries designed to support this conspiracy against me!"

But his protests were drowned out by a commotion near the courthouse entrance. The doors burst open to admit a group of men in the uniform of Scotland Yard, led by a stern-faced inspector whom Poppy recognized from Lady Agnes's descriptions.

"Inspector Bradbury," the judge acknowledged. "What brings you here?"

"New evidence, my lord," the inspector replied, approaching the bench with obvious urgency. "Evidence that corroborates everything Lady Agnes Taverner has just testified to."

He carried a large leather case which he opened to reveal stacks of documents, ledgers, and correspondence. "We have just completed a raid on Lord Redmayne's private offices and residences. What we discovered there confirms a conspiracy reaching into the highest levels of government and society."

The courtroom erupted in excited murmurs as the inspector began displaying the seized materials. Financial records showing systematic fraud, correspondence with corrupt officials, and most damning of all, detailed plans for eliminating witnesses and suppressing evidence.

"Among the documents," Inspector Bradbury continued, "we found specific instructions for the deaths of Sir Charles Hartwell, Sebastian Taverner, and the destruction of Tavener Hall All were ordered by Lord Redmayne as threats to his network's security."

Poppy felt tears streaming down her cheeks as she finally heard official confirmation of what they had suspected all along. Her father had been murdered, as had Sebastian and dear, brave Lucy. Their deaths had not been accidents or coincidences, but calculated acts of violence designed to protect a criminal conspiracy.

"Furthermore," the inspector added, "we have evidence of Lord Redmayne's true identity. The man sitting in this courtroom is not the legitimate holder of the title he claims. His real name is Thomas Wood, a former clerk who assumed the identity of the true Lord Redmayne after arranging that gentleman's death some fifteen years ago."

The revelation sent shockwaves through the assembled crowd. If true, it meant that everything about Redmayne's position in society was built on lies and murder.

"This is madness!" the man claiming to be Redmayne protested, but his voice had taken on a desperate edge. "A tissue of lies designed to destroy an innocent man!"

"Then you won't object to submitting to examination by those who knew the real Lord Redmayne," Inspector Bradbury replied smoothly. "We have several witnesses prepared to testify that you are indeed Thomas Blackwood, not the peer you claim to be."

As if summoned by his words, an elderly woman entered the courtroom, leaning heavily on a walking stick but moving with unmistakable determination. Despite her advanced age, there was something regal about her bearing that commanded immediate attention.

"That," she announced in a voice that carried clearly throughout the room, "is not my nephew."

Lord Justice Blackwood leaned forward with obvious interest. "And you are, madam?"

"Lady Charlotte Redmayne, dowager countess and aunt to the late Lord Redmayne. The real Lord Redmayne, that is, who died in what I was told was a hunting accident some fifteen years ago."

She pointed a trembling finger at the man who had claimed her nephew's identity. "That man was my nephew's secretary, Thomas Wood. He disappeared shortly after my nephew's death, taking with him several valuable items from the estate. I always suspected he was responsible for the tragedy, but I could never prove it."

The courtroom had fallen completely silent as the magnitude of the deception became clear. Not only had the man they knew as Lord Redmayne built his empire on fraud and murder, but his very identity was a lie stolen from his victim.

"Furthermore," Lady Charlotte continued, "I can confirm that Miss Catherine Ashford—now Lady Catherine Hartwell—is indeed the rightful heir to the Ashford estates. My nephew had no legitimate claim to those properties, and neither does this impostor."

The pieces of the puzzle were finally falling into place with devastating clarity. Poppy was not merely investigating inheritance fraud—she was confronting the man who had murdered her father to prevent the exposure of a criminal conspiracy that reached back decades.

"I believe," Jonathan Hartley said, rising from his seat in the gallery, "that we are witnessing the exposure of one of the most extensive criminal conspiracies in recent memory. A conspiracy that has corrupted our legal system, our government, and our society itself."

As he spoke, Poppy noticed that many of those in the courtroom were now looking at her with something approaching awe. She had gone from being a desperate criminal to a heroic figure who had risked everything to expose the truth.

"The courage shown by Miss Hartwell, Mr. Taverner, and Lady Agnes in pursuing this investigation," Hartley continued, "has revealed corruption that might otherwise have remained hidden for generations. They deserve our gratitude, not our condemnation."

The false Redmayne was now clearly desperate, his eyes darting around the courtroom as he sought some means of escape. But Inspector Bradbury's men had positioned themselves at every exit, and there was nowhere to run.

"You have no authority to arrest me!" he shouted. "I am a peer of the realm! I demand to be tried by my peers in the House of Lords!"

"Thomas Wood," Inspector Bradbury said formally, "you are under arrest for murder, fraud, conspiracy, and treason against the Crown. You have no title, no standing, and no protection under the law."

As the constables moved to place him in custody, the man who had terrorized them for so long finally showed his true nature. Gone was the dignified nobleman, replaced by a snarling criminal who fought against his captors with vicious desperation.

"This isn't over!" he screamed as he was dragged toward the exit. "You think you've won, but there are others! The network is larger than you know!"

His threats were lost in the chaos as the courtroom erupted in celebration. Poppy found herself surrounded by well-wishers and supporters, while Edward was finally freed from his shackles and able to embrace her properly for the first time in days.

"It's over," he whispered against her hair. "Finally, it's truly over."

But even as she savoured the moment of victory,

Poppy couldn't shake the feeling that Wood's final words contained a grain of truth. They had exposed one criminal, but how many others remained hidden in the shadows of power?

Lady Agnes approached them, her face bearing an expression of profound relief mixed with exhaustion. "Justice has been served," she said simply. "Sebastian, my father and Lucy can finally rest in peace."

Lord Justice Blackwood called for order one final time as he prepared to dismiss the charges against them. "In light of the evidence presented today," he announced, "it is clear that Miss Hartwell and Mr. Taverner are not criminals but rather heroes who risked everything to expose a conspiracy against justice itself."

As the courtroom slowly emptied, Poppy found herself standing with Edward and Lady Agnes in the dock that had so recently held them as prisoners. Now it felt more like a platform from which they had launched a revolution against corruption and lies.

The battle was won, but she knew that the war for justice would continue. There would always be those who sought to profit from others' misfortune, who would use power and influence to suppress the truth.

But they had proven that even the most powerful conspiracies could be brought down by ordinary people who refused to accept injustice as inevitable.

CHAPTER 20

The euphoria of their courtroom victory was short-lived. Even as Poppy found herself embraced by supporters and celebrated by the press, she couldn't shake the memory of Thomas Wood's final warning about the network being larger than they knew. His words proved prophetic when, three days after his arrest, he was found dead in his cell at Newgate Prison—officially a suicide, though the circumstances raised troubling questions.

"Poison," Inspector Bradbury confirmed grimly when he met with Poppy, Edward, and Lady Agnes at Belmont House. "The same type used in the attempt on Mr. Aldridge's life during the trial.

Someone wanted to ensure Wood could never reveal the full extent of his conspiracy."

"Then there are others," Edward said, his expression troubled. "People who were willing to kill to protect their secrets."

"Undoubtedly. Wood's network included members of Parliament, judges, clerks in government offices, even some within Scotland Yard itself. Exposing him was only the beginning."

Despite the ongoing danger, there had been cause for celebration in the Hartwell household. Rose's engagement to James Whitmore had been quietly restored once the truth about Poppy's innocence became public, and Lady Catherine's health had improved dramatically upon learning that her family's reputation was not only cleared but enhanced by their fight for justice.

"You've become quite the heroine," Rose said with obvious pride as she helped Poppy prepare for what promised to be a momentous evening. "The newspapers are calling you 'The Lady Who Brought Down Lord Redmayne.'"

"I prefer to think of myself as someone who simply refused to accept injustice," Poppy replied, adjusting the sapphire necklace that had belonged to her grandmother. Tonight would mark her first public appearance since the trial, at a reception being held in their honour by reform-minded members of Parliament.

"Still," Rose continued, her eyes sparkling with mischief, "I suspect Mr. Taverner sees you as rather more than a crusader for justice. When are you going to make your actual engagement official?"

The question brought heat to Poppy's cheeks. In all the chaos following their vindication, she and Edward had barely had time to discuss their personal future. Their false engagement had become so real in every way that mattered, yet they had never formally acknowledged what had grown between them.

The reception was being held at Grosvenor House, and as their carriage approached the grand entrance, Poppy was amazed to see crowds of well-wishers lining the street. People called out words of support and applause as she and Edward stepped down, no longer the desperate fugitives they had been just days before.

"Look how far we've come," Edward murmured as they climbed the steps arm in arm. "From the Tower of London to a celebration in Mayfair."

Inside, the reception was a gathering of London's reform-minded elite—politicians who had long suspected corruption in high places, journalists who had championed the cause of justice, and society figures who were eager to associate themselves with the victorious crusade against crime.

Jonathan Hartley approached them almost immediately, his notebook nowhere in sight for once. "Miss Hartwell, Mr. Taverner, I wanted to thank you personally. Your courage has opened doors that seemed permanently sealed. The story of Blackwood's network is just beginning to unfold."

"What have you discovered?" Poppy asked.

"Evidence of corruption reaching back decades. Forged documents, bribed officials, murdered witnesses—it appears that Blackwood's method of operation was to identify wealthy families with complex inheritance issues and then systematically eliminate legitimate heirs while installing his own associates as beneficiaries."

"How many families were affected?"

"We've identified at least a dozen so far, probably more. Your father's investigation was more comprehensive than even you realized—he had been tracking patterns of suspicious deaths and disappeared inheritances across half of England."

As they spoke, Poppy noticed a commotion near the entrance of the reception hall. A man had entered whose presence seemed to create a ripple of unease among the assembled guests. She recognized him as Mr. Crowhurst, the nervous clerk who had delivered the blackmail letters that had started their entire ordeal.

"What is he doing here?" Edward asked, his voice tight with suspicion.

Before anyone could answer, Crowhurst began moving purposefully through the crowd, his hand reaching inside his coat. In that instant, Poppy realized with horrible clarity that Blackwood's network was making one final, desperate attempt to eliminate the witnesses who had destroyed their conspiracy.

"Edward, look out!" she cried, but Crowhurst was already pulling a pistol from his jacket.

The reception erupted in screams and chaos as guests scattered in all directions. Edward threw himself forward, tackling Crowhurst before he could take aim, and the two men crashed to the floor in a desperate struggle.

The pistol discharged into the ceiling, raining plaster down on the struggling figures. Crowhurst proved stronger than his nervous demeanour had suggested, fighting with the desperation of a man who knew his life depended on completing his mission.

"You destroyed everything!" he snarled as he grappled with Edward. "Years of work, decades of planning—all ruined by your meddling!"

"Good," Edward replied grimly, managing to pin Crowhurst's gun hand against the marble floor.

But the clerk had not come alone. As Poppy looked around the chaos-filled room, she spotted other figures moving with purpose through the panicking crowd. The remaining members of Wood's network had come to eliminate everyone who could testify against them.

Inspector Bradbury and his men, who had been present as guests, were already moving to intercept the assassins. But in the confusion, it was difficult to distinguish friend from foe.

"Miss Hartwell!" a voice called out, and Poppy turned to see Lady Agnes pushing through the crowd toward her. "You must get away from here. There are too many of them—"

Her words were cut off as another shot rang out. Lady Agnes stumbled, her hand going to her shoulder where blood was beginning to seep through her dark gown.

"Agnes!" Poppy rushed to support the older woman, who was already struggling to remain standing.

"I'm all right," Lady Agnes gasped. "But you must listen to me. Crowhurst isn't the real threat—he's just a distraction. The man behind all of this, Wood's true partner, is someone none of us suspected."

"Who?"

Before Lady Agnes could answer, a new voice cut through the din of the reception hall.

"I'm afraid Lady Agnes won't be able to complete that revelation."

Poppy turned in horror to see Mr. Bradshaw, Wood's chief lieutenant, standing behind them with a pistol trained on Lady Agnes's heart. But it was the identity of the man beside him that made her blood run cold.

Inspector Bradbury himself stood there, no longer the heroic police officer who had saved them in court, but revealed as the corrupt official who had been protecting Blackwood's network from within Scotland Yard.

"Inspector," Poppy whispered, her voice barely audible over the ongoing chaos. "But you helped us. You provided the evidence that exposed Blackwood."

"I provided carefully selected evidence that eliminated a liability," Bradbury corrected with cold satisfaction. "Thomas Wood had become too reckless, too visible. His arrest served our purposes better than his continued freedom."

"You used us," Edward said, his voice filled with horrified understanding. He had managed to subdue Crowhurst but was now faced with the realization that their apparent victory had been orchestrated by their true enemies.

"We used your investigation to eliminate threats to our network while appearing to champion justice," Bradbury confirmed. "Wood's downfall has actually strengthened our position—we're now free to operate without his unpredictable interference."

Lady Agnes struggled to speak despite her wound. "The network... it goes higher than we thought. Members of Parliament, judges, even..."

"Even the Home Secretary himself," Bradbury finished with obvious satisfaction. "Did you really think a conspiracy of this magnitude could operate without protection from the very highest levels of government?"

The revelation was staggering. They had exposed one criminal only to discover that he was merely a middle manager in a conspiracy that reached into the heart of British government itself.

"What do you want?" Poppy asked, though she dreaded the answer.

"What we have always wanted—silence. Lady Agnes's testimony has been... problematic. Your continued investigation threatens to expose elements of our network that must remain hidden. The solution is simple: you must all be silenced permanently."

"Here? In front of hundreds of witnesses?"

"Tragic deaths during a terrorist attack by anarchists seeking to destroy the established order," Bradshaw explained with chilling calm. "Several explosive devices were discovered after the fact, along with radical literature linking the attack to foreign agitators. Very convenient for justifying increased security measures and reduced civil liberties."

As he spoke, Poppy became aware of other figures moving through the reception hall—men placing what appeared to be small packages in strategic locations. The scope of their plan was becoming horrifyingly clear.

"You're going to murder everyone here," she said.

"Everyone who matters," Bradbury corrected. "The reformers, the journalists, the politicians who have been asking inconvenient questions. A single night's work will eliminate our most persistent opponents while providing justification for the authoritarian measures we require."

But even as despair threatened to overwhelm her, Poppy noticed something that gave her hope. Edward was slowly manoeuvring himself into position behind Bradbury, while several of the other guests—far from being helpless victims—were revealing themselves to be armed and prepared.

Jonathan Hartley emerged from behind an overturned table, a pistol in his hand and a grim smile on his face. "Inspector Bradbury, you're under arrest for conspiracy, murder, and treason against the Crown."

"On whose authority?" Bradbury sneered.

"On the authority of Her Majesty's Special Branch," a new voice announced from the entrance to the hall. "And in the name of the Queen herself."

A dozen men in the uniforms of the Royal Guard entered the reception hall, their weapons trained on Bradbury and his associates. Leading them was a figure that made even the corrupt inspector's face pale with recognition.

"Sir Marcus Wellington," Bradbury whispered. "But you're supposed to be in India."

"Reports of my colonial service have been greatly exaggerated," the newcomer replied with cold authority. "I've actually been investigating corruption within the Metropolitan Police for the past six months. Your network's activities have been under surveillance far longer than you realize."

As the Royal Guards moved to secure the scene, Poppy felt the last pieces of the puzzle falling into place. Their investigation had been watched and guided from the beginning, but not by their enemies —by forces within the government itself who were working to expose and eliminate the corruption that had infected British institutions.

"It's finally over," Edward said, helping her to her feet as the immediate danger passed.

"Yes," Poppy replied, looking around at the aftermath of their final confrontation. "But at what cost?"

The network had been exposed and its leaders arrested, but the damage done over the years—the lives lost, the families destroyed, the trust in British institutions shattered—would take far longer to repair.

Still, as she watched Inspector Bradbury and his associates being led away in chains, Poppy felt a deep satisfaction. Justice had finally been served, even if it had taken longer and cost more than anyone had anticipated.

EPILOGUE

$\mathcal{E}\!\mathcal{B}$

SIX MONTHS LATER

*T*he morning sun streamed through tall windows, illuminating the restored grandeur of rooms that had been left to decay under decades of fraudulent stewardship. Poppy stood at the window of what had once been the library, watching as workmen completed the final repairs to the estate's Gothic chapel where, in just two hours, she would become Mrs. Edward Taverner in truth as well as in the affections they had discovered during their perilous masquerade.

"You look pensive for a bride on her wedding morning," Lady Agnes observed as she entered the room, moving with only the slightest stiffness from the shoulder wound she had sustained during the final confrontation with Bradshaw's network.

"I was thinking about justice," Poppy replied, turning from the window. "How much we achieved, and yet how much remains undone."

The past six months had brought sweeping changes to British society. The exposure of the corruption network had triggered investigations reaching into every level of government, resulting in dozens of arrests and the implementation of new oversight measures designed to prevent such systematic abuse of power. Yet Poppy knew that for every criminal they had exposed, others remained hidden in the shadows.

"Inspector Bradbury's trial begins next week," Lady Agnes said, settling into one of the newly reupholstered chairs. "Sir Marcus Wellington assures me that the evidence against him is overwhelming."

"And the others?"

"The Home Secretary resigned in disgrace, though he claims ignorance of the network's activities. Three Members of Parliament have been arrested, along with a dozen clerks and minor officials. The Lord Chancellor has announced sweeping reforms to prevent such corruption in the future."

It was progress, certainly, but Poppy couldn't help thinking of all those who had paid the ultimate price for the truth—her father, Sebastian, and most painfully, young Lucy, whose bright spirit had been extinguished just as she was beginning to discover her own courage.

"She would have been so excited about today," Lady Agnes said softly, following Poppy's thoughts with the intuitive understanding that had grown between them. "Lucy always believed that love would triumph over adversity. She would have delighted in seeing you and Edward find happiness together."

"I wish she could have been here to see it," Poppy replied, her voice thick with emotion.

"Perhaps she is, in her own way."

The door opened to admit Rose, radiant in her role as maid of honour despite having been married herself just three months earlier. Her own wedding to James Whitmore had been a much quieter affair, held while the investigations were still ongoing, but no less joyful for its simplicity.

"Poppy, you must come and get ready," Rose announced with the authority of someone who had successfully navigated her own wedding preparations. "Mother is beside herself with worry that we'll be late, and Edward has been pacing the morning room for the past hour."

"Edward is here?" Poppy asked with surprise. "Surely he should be at the church by now."

"He claims he needs to speak with you about some urgent matter concerning the estate," Rose replied with obvious exasperation. "I told him it could wait until after the ceremony, but he was quite insistent."

Poppy exchanged a glance with Lady Agnes, who shrugged with amused resignation. "Edward has always been one to worry about details. Perhaps you should see what's troubling him."

She found him in the morning room, dressed in his wedding attire but looking uncharacteristically nervous. The past months had been kind to him— the restoration of his reputation and the resolution of his guilt over Sebastian's death had returned much of the confidence that had first attracted her to him.

"Edward," she said gently, "what's so urgent that it couldn't wait another few hours?"

"This," he replied, producing a letter from his coat pocket. "It arrived this morning by special courier from London."

The letter bore the seal of the Crown Prosecution Service, and as Poppy read its contents, her eyes widened with amazement.

"A royal commendation for services to justice," she read aloud. "And an invitation to advise the government on new measures to prevent corruption in the inheritance system."

"They want both of us," Edward said. "To serve as special investigators with authority to examine suspicious cases and recommend reforms."

The offer was everything they had worked toward—official recognition of their efforts and the opportunity to continue fighting the injustices they had exposed. Yet Poppy found herself hesitating.

"It would mean spending much of our time in London," she said slowly. "Away from the estate, away from the quiet life we've been planning."

"It would," Edward agreed. "But it would also mean that Lucy's death—all their deaths—would serve a lasting purpose. We could help ensure that no other families suffer as ours have."

She studied his face, seeing the conflict there between his desire for peace and his commitment to justice. It was the same conflict she felt within herself.

"What do you want to do?" she asked.

"I want to marry you," he said simply. "Everything else we can decide together."

The ceremony itself was smaller than it might

have been under different circumstances, attended primarily by family and the allies they had gathered during their fight against corruption. Jonathan Hartley was there, having become something of a celebrity among reform-minded journalists. Sir Marcus Wellington attended in his capacity as the government's chief investigator of institutional corruption. Even Mr. Aldridge had come, recovered from his poisoning and eager to contribute to the new oversight measures being implemented.

As Poppy walked down the aisle of the small chapel, her arm linked with that of her mother, she was struck by the contrast with the false engagement that had brought her and Edward together. Then, they had been playing roles for the benefit of society's expectations. Now, they were making promises that came from the deepest parts of their hearts.

"Do you, Poppy Catherine Hartwell, take this man to be your lawfully wedded husband?" the rector asked.

"I do," she replied, her voice clear and strong.

"And do you, Edward Samuel Taverner, take this woman to be your lawfully wedded wife?"

"I do," Edward said, his pale eyes never leaving her face.

As they exchanged rings—the simple band

replacing the sapphire engagement ring that had marked the beginning of their deception—Poppy felt the weight of everything they had endured together settling into something precious and permanent.

The wedding breakfast was held in the restored great hall of Ashford Manor, the walls lined with portraits of Poppy's ancestors who had been wrong-fully dispossessed by Blackwood's conspiracy. It felt fitting to celebrate their union in the place where her family's rightful heritage had finally been restored.

"So," Rose said as they stood together watching the dancing, "have you decided about the govern-ment's offer?"

"We have," Poppy replied, her hand finding Edward's automatically. "We're going to accept it."

"All of it?"

"The advisory position, yes. The investigation work, partially. We'll spend half our time in London working on reforms, and half our time here, rebuilding what was lost."

It was a compromise that satisfied both their desire for justice and their need for peace. They would continue fighting corruption, but they would also create something positive from the ashes of their ordeal.

As the afternoon wore on, guests began to depart, offering congratulations and promises to support their future endeavours. Lady Agnes was among the last to leave, embracing them both with the fierce affection of someone who had found redemption through their forgiveness.

"Take care of each other," she said simply. "And remember that some victories are worth any price."

That evening, as they stood together on the terrace overlooking the restored gardens of Ashford Manor, Poppy and Edward reflected on the journey that had brought them to this moment.

"Do you ever regret it?" Edward asked. "Everything we went through, everything we lost?"

"I regret the price others paid," Poppy replied thoughtfully. "But I don't regret the fight itself. We proved that even the most powerful conspiracies can be brought down by ordinary people who refuse to accept injustice."

"And we found each other in the process."

"Yes," she agreed, leaning into his embrace. "We found each other."

As they watched the sun set over the estate that had finally been returned to its rightful owners, a new sound reached them from the village below. Church bells were ringing—not the solemn tolling for the dead that had marked so much of their recent experience, but the joyful celebration of new beginnings.

The future stretched before them, full of challenges but also full of hope. There would be more corruption to expose, more injustices to fight, more battles to win in the endless struggle for truth and justice. But they would face those challenges together, armed with the knowledge that love and determination could overcome even the most entrenched evil.

In the distance, a lone owl called from the depths of the ancient forest that bordered the estate—the same haunting cry that had once filled Poppy with foreboding during her first night at Taverner Hall. Now, it seemed like a song of victory, a reminder that even in the darkest times, hope persisted.

The darkness of corruption might be vast and deep, but it could not withstand the light of truth when that light was carried by those brave enough to hold it steady against the storm.

As they turned to go inside their restored home, Poppy caught sight of something that made her pause. There, pinned to the door frame, was a small piece of paper—anonymous, unsigned, but unmistakably deliberate in its placement.

It is not over.

The words sent a chill through her, a reminder that their victory, however complete it seemed, had not eliminated all their enemies. Somewhere in the shadows, others waited and watched, ready to continue the work that Wood and Bradbury had begun.

Edward followed her gaze and read the message, his expression growing grim. For a moment, the peace of their wedding day was threatened by the spectre of future dangers.

But then Poppy deliberately removed the note, crumpled it in her hand, and dropped it to the ground.

"Perhaps not," she said firmly. "But we are ready for whatever comes next."

Together, they stepped across the threshold of their home, leaving the anonymous threat behind them in the darkness where it belonged. Whatever shadows might gather in the future, they would face them as they had faced all their previous challenges —together, and with the absolute conviction that justice would ultimately prevail.

The door closed behind them with a solid, reassuring sound, shutting out the night and all its uncertainties. But even as they settled into the warmth and safety of their restored home, both knew that their greatest adventures—and their most important battles—still lay ahead.

The End

Printed in Dunstable, United Kingdom